Suburban Monsters

Christopher Hawkins

Coronis Publishing

"Green Eyes" appears for the first time in this volume.

"Moonrise Over Water With Sargassum, 2022. Oil on Canvas" appears for the first time in this volume.

"Storms of the Present" first appeared on the *Tales to Terrify* podcast, episode #469, January 2021.

"Origin Story" first appeared in *Night Terrors II*, Blood Bound Books, 2012.

"Poppy" first appeared in *Kids Are Hell!*, Hellbound Books, September 2022.

"Interlude" first appeared on the *Cast of Wonders* podcast, episode #515, November 2022.

"The Stumblybum Imperative" first appeared in Fusion Fragment #5, March 2021.

"Shadowman" appears for the first time in this volume.

"Carpenter's Thumb" first appeared online in *The Harrow*, March 2007.

"Swallow" first appeared in *The Big Book of New Short Horror*, Pill Hill Press, 2011.

"Ten and Gone" first appeared in Underland Arcana #3, Summer 2021.

"Notice" first appeared in *Lovecraftiana*, Lammas Eve 2021.

"A Candle for the Birthday Boy" first appeared in Read by Dawn vol 2, Bloody Books, 2007.

Cover design by Fay Lane

First Printing - March, 2023

Praise for Suburban Monsters

"A masterfully written collection of dark and uniquely disquieting tales. Some tales collected here are bizarre and whimsical. Others are distressing and uncomfortable. Regardless, each tale is brilliantly tethered by an absolute truth: there is darkness lurking inside each person you pass on the street. Peel back the gristle and behold the exquisite void waiting for you beneath the skin..."

Eric LaRocca, author of *Things Have Gotten Worse Since We Last Spoke and Other Misfortunes*

"Each of the stories in SUBURBAN MONSTERS is a masterful exercise in building tension and creating a sense of unease, as author Christopher Hawkins delves into the dark, twisted inner lives of characters who may not be all they seem."

IndieReader (Starred Review)

"Human fiends and supernatural ones collide in Hawkins' *Suburban Monsters*. Shows us that beneath any facade of normalcy, strange things lurk, just waiting to sink their teeth in. Christopher Hawkins loves turning over rocks and showing us the grotesque, squirming things underneath, and you'll have a hard time looking away."

Brian Asman, author of Man, Fuck This House

"Reading Christopher Hawkins' *Suburban Monsters* is like walking down a street in a dark neighborhood at night with the windows lit and curtains, some of them, parted. Terrible things go on inside, but out here you're safe, except then there's a soft sound behind you, and then another. The faces in all those windows turn, and you are seen."

Christi Nogle, author of *Beulah*

"An assortment of jolts, abominations, and shaken nerves that readers won't soon forget."

Kirkus Reviews

"Harrowing and irresistible. A terrific collection of short stories that unmasks the horror lurking in everyday humanity. You'll never look at your neighbors in the same way again."

Brian Pinkerton, author of *The Nirvana Effect*

"These are more than horror stories; these are little word grenades that roll quietly into the closet of your mind... only to explode later! I may never forget the last lines of "A Candle For The Birthday Boy," perhaps the perfect closer to this incendiary collection. Read at your own risk."

John Everson, Bram Stoker Award-winning author of *Five Deaths for Seven Songbirds* and *Night Where*

"Hawkins's bold premises and deft followthrough create gut-wrenching tension sure to thrill horror enthusiasts... Throughout, visceral imagery brings the terror to life: readers will hear the "wet gurgle" and see the "blossom of brownish red" liquid spreading out. Killer opening lines such as "It was the blood that changed everything" make the twisted and ominous worlds inviting."

Booklife

"This book is not for the faint of heart, as it will take you on a roller coaster of emotions with each twist and turn of the page. I would highly recommend *Suburban Monsters* to anyone who is looking for a captivating and chilling read. The writing is exceptional, with each story offering a unique perspective on the darker side of suburban life. Whether you're a seasoned horror fan or just starting to explore the genre, this book is sure to leave a lasting impression."

Reedsy Discovery

For Kris

Contents

Green Eyes

Danny Chambers said that I was dirty and that I was poor, so I pushed him down on the ground. He said mean things about Mama too, things that I didn't understand. *Grownup* things. I knew they were extra-bad from the way his friends were all laughing, so I got on top of him and hit him in the nose until his blood came out. He didn't say anything about me or about Mama after that. He just looked up at me with the scared in his eyes until his friends pulled me off of him and he tripped all over his feet trying to run away.

It was the blood that got me sent to the counselor's office, but it wasn't my fault this time. Danny made me do it, with his stupid donkey laugh and his big dumb white teeth. I'd cut my finger on those teeth. Little beads of red came up over the skin when I squeezed. But Miss Elburn doesn't care about my blood. She only cares about his. I can see her in her office through the glass with her stern face on, trying to call Mama like she had the time I was late for school, and the time before that, and the time before that. I told her that our phone didn't work anymore but she never believes me, even though I always tell the truth. I know she's getting ready to yell at me again, so I don't stay long enough to let her. You don't have to stay. That's the part they never tell kids. They don't even lock the doors.

I run past the parking lot down the little two-lane road and I don't look back until all the buildings are gone and all I can see are the wildflowers growing up from the drainage ditches and the broken wooden fences that run along the road in crooked little lines. My sandals slap against my heels, so I kick them off as I go. I only wore them for school and I won't be going back to that place anymore anyway. The pavement is hot, but I'm moving too fast for it to burn my feet.

My house is my favorite place in the whole world because the whole yard is grown over with wildflowers and stalks of thistle that are taller than I am. They've grown up all over the little dirt path that used to lead to the steps, but I know my way around them. The little thorns and sticker bushes never even grab at my dress. It's my good yellow dress that I'm wearing–the best one I have–and when I look down at it, I see that it really is dirty. There are smudges all over it and the hem is torn. I still don't feel bad about hitting Danny Chambers though, because Danny Chambers always deserves it.

But my house is my favorite because I can lie on my back in the front room at night and see the stars through the hole in the roof. There's grass that's grown up between the floorboards and wide, soft leaves that make it like lying on cool sheets, and sometimes I fall asleep right there and sleep all the way until the morning. But mostly, my house is my favorite place because that's where my mama is. The front door sticks and scrapes a little when I open it, so I know that she knows I'm home early.

I hear a thump and I can tell that she's moving around behind her bedroom door.

Miss Elburn made the police come to my house once. I don't know it was Miss Elburn who made them for sure, but I still know it. That was the day that Billy Durley told me to eat a grasshopper on a dare and I ate a whole handful because grasshoppers are yummy and I eat them all the time. I crunched them all up right in his face and when he cried they sent me to Miss Elburn's office and she asked me a bunch of questions about why I didn't bring a lunch and when was the last time I had a bath and does my house have electricity. I didn't answer, because Miss Elburn was asking like she already knew the answers, and it wasn't like any of it was Miss Elburn's business anyway.

When I got home that day, there was a police car at the end of the gravel driveway, but its lights weren't even on. A man and a woman with guns and blue uniforms were standing on the dirt path. Mama was on the porch, all frowny with her arms crossed. Mama was sick. This was before she got real sick, but it was still weird to see her out of her bed and in her robe with her hair going every which way. I hid in the tall grass by where the fence fell over and listened to them talk about *endangerment* and *neglect* and a whole bunch of other things I didn't understand. Mama understood though, because Mama got real quiet then and didn't talk anymore until they went away. Even from the grass, I could see that her face was turning red, and when she went back to the house she started to cough so much that I didn't think she'd ever stop.

Mama was sick all the time back then, but she's better now. She almost never came out of her room again after the police came, though. I used to have to bring her water from the faucet in a big cup until the faucet stopped making water and then I had to bring it in a bucket all the way from the creek. I had to be careful every time and make sure I stepped over the big circle of little leafs and crushed seeds that she'd made around her bed. I knew breaking the circle was bad, but Mama never told me why. When she could talk, she told me I was her good girl. I asked her if the police were coming to take me away and her face got dark and she told me she'd never let that happen. Not ever.

I was sick once, too. I had a fever of *a hundred and six degrees* and Mama told me later that I almost died! Mama made me all better, though. She pulled up things from our garden and peeled off bark from the trees in the forest behind our house. She crushed them up in a little bowl and poured hot water on them and made me drink it up. It tasted like garlic and honey and smelled like dead leaves after a rain, and even though I made a yucky face, she made me drink it all. The next day it was like I'd never even had a fever! I wanted to make Mama all better by crushing up leafs too, but she told me it wasn't the same kind of sick. I knew by how she said it that she really meant that it was a *worse* sick. A *real bad* sick. Mama talked a lot back then, and she told me I could help her when the time was right. I like to help. I'm good at helping.

After the faucet stopped making water the lights stopped working, too. The food in the refrigerator got smelly so I left it closed and didn't open it again. But that was okay because the reeds and thistle in the yard were tall by then and the grasshoppers were everywhere! There were breaks in the fences where I could find blueberries and corn, and down the block Mrs. Gantner's garden sometimes had tomatoes. The mail kept coming though, every day except the days I didn't go to school. I tried staying home from school to try to make the mail stop, but it kept coming anyway.

I used to try to read the letters to Mama when they came, but mostly I just sat on the floor of her room and listened to her breathing. It was low and crackly, like something was loose inside her chest, and sometimes it would stop and I would hold my own breath until she started up again. I'd sit inside the circle with my back against the bed and read the letters to her while she was sleeping. I always left off the ones from Child Protective Services. Those I only read quiet to myself. Sometimes there was knocking at the door and I'd make fists and squeeze my eyes shut and wish for it to go away.

When Mama stopped breathing for good though, I wasn't scared. She'd already told me exactly what to do. She told me around the time her coughs started getting real bad and she made me say it all back to her every day so I wouldn't forget. That was a long time ago, but I still remember all of it. Make a fire in the fireplace. Boil the water in the pot. Take the pouch from Mama's nightstand and empty it in the jar. Pour the water on top. Don't drop it. Don't spill. It was easy, and the seeds in Mama's room had grown up all over the bed and down through the floor and into the ground, so I didn't have to worry anymore about breaking the circle. I put the jar by her mouth and made her drink it all up. Even though she made a yucky face, I made her drink it all.

After a while Mama's chest got all still and I couldn't hear anything crackling inside anymore, so I took the big seed with all the spiky prickers on it and closed it up inside her mouth just like she said. When she told me that part, I asked her if it was going to hurt and she told me no. She must have been right because she didn't yell out or cry or anything, even when I pushed up on her chin and heard the seed go crunch.

I went to school just like normal the next day, and a bunch of days after that. Back when she could still talk, Mama said that it was important that I go to school, even if I didn't feel like it. She wouldn't tell me why. Even when I told her that I hated school and didn't want to go, she wouldn't tell me. But I already knew why, because I'd read all the letters, even the ones that I hadn't read out loud to Mama.

Every day when I got home I'd lay next to her on her bed full of leafs. I told her about how Miss Bodington was teaching us fractions and how I caught Danny Chambers looking at me all weird and moony when he thought I couldn't see. Mama would listen and I'd hug onto her tight, even when her body got skinny, even when her ribs got all covered in moss and I could see all the way through them. She never said anything but I knew she heard me because she was smiling. I could see all her teeth.

At night I lay in the front room and looked up at the stars. I listened to the grasshoppers singing in the yard and the soft shifting sound that mama made behind her bedroom door. I listened to the wind rustling through the thistle and the tall grass and I was happy, because I was home.

Now the police are back. Miss Elburn must have been talking to them the whole time I was outside her office because they got here really quick. I hear their car door slam and their shoes crunch on gravel and dry leaves. I hear their voices all muffled, saying things about our home, saying things about Mama. Sad things. Even a few mean things. Mama hears them too, because a loud thump comes from behind her door and I hear rushing noises from under the floorboards that sound like a nest of snakes.

The voices are getting closer, and I can hear them yelling and making swears because they don't know the way past the sticker bushes and thorns. I hear a sound like the wind through the grass, only there is no wind and the sound is so loud that it's almost like howling. There's a big thump, the sound of something heavy being dragged. The swears are screams now, but they don't scare me at all. I still get up and go to Mama's room though, and I close the door behind me.

Mama is sitting up in her bed. The whole room is green now, with vines all the way down the walls and across the floor and falling over the bed like great big ropes. Mama's looking at me and she's green too, but the greenest green is inside her eyes. Outside, a gun makes a loud bang. I hear a crunch, all wet like breaking celery, and then no one's screaming anymore. The whole world gets quiet and it's just me and Mama again. She looks down at me and I can see her heart all spiky like a sticker seed in her chest, and it's beating. It's beating just for me.

Moonrise Over Water With Sargassum, 2022. Oil On Canvas

IT WAS THE BLOOD that changed everything.

They had gone down to the beach to watch the moon come up over the water. Paul was in the lead because Paul was always in the lead, a bottle of Bollinger–his third–dangling from one hand as he swayed, tripping down the little boardwalk in his bare feet. Callie followed along behind him, close enough to be seen but not close enough to reach. Paul could get handsy when he drank–and often enough when he didn't–and she didn't want to be within grabbing distance. She carried her heels in one hand, picking her steps, pulling her shawl close around her shoulders to stave off the chill of the night air.

She hadn't wanted to come outside, but when had that ever mattered? She hadn't even wanted the Champagne, but Paul had insisted because he didn't want to have to drink alone. They were celebrating, after all. He hadn't told her why. Some new building contract, maybe, or a new bit of legislation that added another digit to his portfolio. Or maybe it was only that one of his mistresses' pregnancy tests came back negative.

Callie had long-since stopped caring about such things. She was there to witness, not participate, so she followed, just like she always followed, watching her drunk husband stumble his way down the rocky beach to where the waves met the shore.

The wind blew off the water and brought with it the taste of salt, and beneath that the sour brimstone smell of rotting seaweed. It lay on the beach in dark lumps, long ropes of it stretching out to the sea, bobbing and shifting as the roiling surf heaved it onto the sand. Paul had made a show of apologizing for it the first time he had brought her here, but it was one of the things that had made her fall in love with this place, with him. Together, they'd stood at the water's edge and she'd dug her feet down under the leaves, felt them tickle her toes as the tide came in. They'd fallen down and made love in the surf and the seaweed like something out of a movie and, just like that, she was his. Those were better times. Or were they? She didn't know anymore. The night air and the sound of the ocean had left her feeling wistful. Maybe it was just the champagne.

Paul let out a howl. His back was arched, his arms wide, as if he were challenging the moon to rise. A sliver of it shone over the water, bright, like a promise. She thought about painting it, then pushed the thought aside. She hadn't painted in weeks. Maybe months. She'd lost track. It was the painting that had brought them together, that had made her stand out to him as a thing to be purchased and possessed. Maybe that was why she'd stopped. He'd been there at her first opening, and bought the centerpiece for twice what she was asking. She'd known who he was, of course. Everyone did. But he'd made her feel like she was the famous one. He'd smiled at her, attentive to her every movement like she was the only woman in the world. He was everything she'd never thought she'd wanted. VIP rooms and private jets. Red carpets and flash bulbs that dazzled her when they called her name.

Now he was standing in the surf with his cock out, the bottle forgotten and bobbing with the waves. He let out an arcing stream of piss that the wind caught and threw back at him, leaving him swearing and sputtering as he staggered back up the beach. She tried not to laugh. *Oh God, don't let him see you laugh.* She'd done that once, in those early days, on another drunken night when the air was too cold for the beach. He'd taken the cheese knife to the painting she'd been working on, slashed it to ribbons. He'd told her that he was the only reason anyone bought her work. He'd told her that she was nothing without him.

Now she only turned away and hoped that he'd forgotten she was even there. Some nights, while he slept, she crept down to the beach and stood in the waves with the seaweed curling about her toes and tried to remember the way he'd once been. Had that person ever been real? Or had she conjured him out of idol worship and wishful thinking? She'd tried to leave him once. More than once. One time she had left her suitcases packed full on the bed, hoping he would find them, hoping it would be enough to make him change. He'd only turned them over and emptied them into a pile on the floor. Without a word, he'd pulled out his phone, pressed a few times and held it out to her.

On the screen was a contact list of every major gallery from New York to L.A. Acquavella. The Gagosian. Kopeikin and Lurie. Numbers for Milan, London, Tokyo. Names she knew and names she hadn't even heard of.

"See how far you get," he'd said, holding the phone out at arms length like he was spraying a bug with a can of poison. "Just see how far."

She hadn't tried again after that. She became docile, a shadow that drifted past the windows of the beach house, trying not to catch his eye. She'd stopped painting altogether. The brushes were his now, things that he controlled, hateful things that she did not want to touch any more than she wanted to touch him. A mere accessory, she followed in his wake, smiling when told, dressing the way he wanted. He wore her the way he wore a watch, a set of cuff-links, and when they were alone he took her off just as easily.

The wind brought her salt and sulfur, and she closed her eyes to inhale it. She listened to the sound of the waves and knew just how she might paint them. Dark blue, almost black. Not a color but the absence of color. That hint of moon in slashes of brilliant white, little dappled promises so intense that they'd dance before your eyes. But for the waves, all was quiet, and she felt the calm that only quiet could bring. In that quiet she could almost imagine the brush in her hand, the soft sweep of bristles on canvas. In the quiet she was happy again because she could not hear him.

She turned, expecting to see Paul pissing downwind, but the beach was empty. In that moment she felt a fleeting thrill at the thought that he might have fallen in the surf, that the waves might have borne him out to sea and out of her life forever. She pushed the thought away as her eyes adjusted to see that he was still there, lying on his back, a dark lump in the sand. There were his bare feet pointed up at the sky, a pale arm stretched over his head. She'd seen him passed out a dozen times, but this wasn't that. There was something in the way one leg was folded beneath the other, in the rag-doll look of him, like he'd been dropped there by some careless child.

She crept to his side, feet slipping on wide tangles of wet weeds, fearing what might happen if he roused, her heart pounding at the thought of what might happen if he didn't. One arm was flung out at his side and his shirt was open. She fell to her knees in the sand next to him, put her hand on his chest to see if he was breathing. His breath was slow and shallow, barely there at all.

And, of course, there was the blood.

It pooled on the seaweed that fanned out beneath his head and soaked a wide, dark patch into the dry sand. There was so much of it, too much of it, running in black rivulets around the fist-sized rock that lay by his ear. She reached out a hand to find the wound, to put pressure on it and stop the bleeding long enough to get back to the house and call for help. She reached out, but she stopped.

A thought unfurled in her mind, gaining shape and color and depth like layers of paint. No one knew they were here. The nearest neighbor was a hundred yards up the beach and around a bend. His howling would have drowned away in the sound of the surf and the wind. The story told itself. They'd been drinking. She fell asleep on the couch. He must have gone down to the beach. Oh, God. Why hadn't he woken her? Why did he have to go down there by himself?

And after that? When all the questions were asked and answered and the flashing lights of the ambulance had gone and the rising tide had washed away all the blood, she'd be free. She could leave this place, this cage, with its glass walls that let her see everything and touch nothing. The blood was freedom. All she had to do was let it flow.

His chest rose and fell, stronger now, or was it only her imagination? She could leave now, leave and not look back and let the tide do the rest. But what if it didn't? Head wounds bled a lot–she knew that–bled so much sometimes that it could look like dying when really it was just a scratch. She could just picture him standing in the doorway, his head matted with blood and sand, his clothes wet with seawater, but only up to his waist, demanding to know why she hadn't helped him.

The waves crashed at her back, louder now, and as they receded so too did her vision of the future. Great stabs of black smeared over bright swaths of yellow and Pthalo Blue. She looked down at her husband, at his hand outstretched, and thought of the sound of the knife slashing through the painting she had made, the painting she had made for him, of him. She thought of the phone and all those numbers, the way he'd held it, just inches from her face, like a loaded gun.

She pulled at his arm and he spun sideways. He was heavy, but not so heavy that she couldn't manage, and the water was only a few steps away. She tugged again and he let out a groan. His fly was still undone and the way the sand gathered against his armpit like a snowdrift made him look small, made her wonder how she'd ever been afraid of him. His body slipped along the ropes of still-wet seaweed, coming easier now. It was only ever his money that gave him size. She'd give as much of it away as she could. She'd only keep just enough, enough to live her own life again. Two million, maybe three. Enough money to never have to think about money again. She'd use the rest to do good things, things that Paul would never dream of doing, if he lived a thousand years. Things that helped other people. Amazing things. Selfless things.

Water lashed at her ankles, and when the waves rode in she let them float him the rest of the way. The surf foamed pink with the blood from his scalp, red and white mixed with a palette knife. A fresh wave tried to heave him back onto the sand, but she held tight to his collar, dragging him out until the water was at her waist and the drifting seaweed brushed at her feet. She let him go, but he only bobbed there stubbornly at her side until the next wave came and she had to grab hold of him to keep him from the shore.

She'd give it all away, she told herself, every last penny of it. She'd leave the beach house and the cars and the tabloids and the jewelry. She'd take nothing but her paints and the clothes on her back and she'd leave and she'd never look back. She'd beg for forgiveness every night if she had to, but she'd beg on her own terms, at the end of each one of her own days, in a life that belonged to her alone. She took hold of his shoulders. His eyes were closed but his lips were moving, muttering something so softly that she could not hear it for the sounds of the sea.

She pushed him down until his head sank beneath the surface, and the words bubbled up, silent, from his open mouth.

The waves rose up to obscure his face, and she was grateful. They brought with them a hush that pushed away the crash of the surf and the sound of her own heartbeat ringing in her ears. But the waves did not go out, and as the water grew still around her, she felt a presence at her back, as if someone was looking over her shoulder. She turned to find the seaweed piled up behind her, rising above the water in a great heap, like some huge head peeking up just over the surface. It kept the waves at bay, and as they crashed against its bulk the weeds tossed and swirled, yellow-brown that glinted green in the moonlight, dancing like hair in a breeze.

It stared at her, and though it had no eyes that she could see she could feel it watching her. Its head seemed to tilt, curious, without judgment, as it regarded her, hunched over with her arms elbow-deep in the black water. She could feel a tension in the thing, an anticipation, a subtle urging that drove her on. A sense of inevitability, as if it knew that it would find her at this place, as if it had been here all along, waiting.

Beneath the water, Paul convulsed, and Callie flinched as his hand rose up to wrap itself around her arm. She could see his face just below the still water, his eyes open now, wide and frightened. His fingers found her throat, but his touch was weak and getting weaker. He was looking right at her, and she felt a little thrill tremble through her limbs because he was finally seeing her, maybe for the first time. She understood at last that this was how it had to end, how she'd known it would end from the moment he'd taken the knife to her work, stabbing at his own face on the canvas. As his eyes lost their focus, she could read in them a final question, not *why?* but *how dare you?*

She felt the faint touch of leafy fronds at her back and when she staggered they kept her upright. The seaweed was all around her now, floating on the calmed water, encircling her, encircling Paul with his eyes still open, staring sightless at the moonlit sky. The wide leaves made a bed beneath him, pale brown fading into blue-black. She let go of him and he sank, and as he drifted down the fronds rose to meet him. They cradled his body, drawing him into their folds, twining around his legs, around his neck. Coiling like snakes, they engulfed him, piling over his body and pulling him into their mass until at last he disappeared, and there was nothing left but the smell of salt and sulfur on the breeze.

Callie turned then, her hands empty now but still held out before her, as if they had not yet realized their burden was gone. The seaweed towered high above her head, long strands dripping like a spill of wet hair across what should have been its face. She felt its calm fall over her, drifting, almost hypnotic, as the weeds closed in around her. They brushed her legs and twined around her middle. She brought them to her face and felt the wetness against her cheeks, bitter and salty, like tears. She felt their satisfaction, their acceptance of her sacrifice, the keeping of a promise she had made to them without even knowing.

The coils fell away then, and in a moment they were gone. Callie watched them go, glints of white moonlight on yellow-green, slinking away into the blue-spotted black, leaving only highlights of white. She watched as the great head receded into the water, losing its shape, dismantled by the pounding surf that once again threatened to sweep her off her feet. She crept to the shore, and with her legs not willing to hold her she fell upon the sand. She sat on the beach with the weeds coiled around her feet, shivering as the breeze dried her. She watched moon trace its arc across the sky, gray-dappled white haloed in a dark and somber blue, to meet the reddening dawn.

Storms of the Present

I WATCH THE DELIVERY man through the gap in the curtains. The sun is bright and it makes me squint. As he bends down to leave the little box by the door I see the muscles of his calves flex. It occurs to me that it must be from all the walking he does, and it occurs to me that I could go walking now too. If I did it enough, I might be able to see my calves flex the way his do. For an instant I picture myself following him down the driveway to the sidewalk and on along it to the place where it ends at the cross-street, where that new and unfamiliar road disappears behind a row of other people's houses. I shudder to think of myself there, looking back at the little house that has been my only home, fearing that I might lose my way back. I relax a little when I see that the man is gone, but I still wait as long as I'm able to before I crack open the door to scoop the package inside.

The box took three days to get here, two more than it had said on the website. This point had been very important to me up until this moment, but now that I have my hands on the thing it seems barely worth remembering. I test the weight of it as I wind my way to the kitchen, stepping carefully around leaning towers of newspapers, past stacks of half-empty boxes. It's no bigger than a pencil case, and I know its contents are right because I can feel them rattling around inside.

I find a knife in the sink that's not too wet and I use it to saw through the packing tape. The smaller box inside is blue and white, just like the picture on the website, and it fits exactly in the place I had left for it, near the scale and the stack of carefully-folded paper towels.

I steel myself and resolve to wait until morning before I go any further. After all, what was one more day compared to the days of waiting, and the days of planning before that? One day wouldn't change my mind, but it would cool my nerves. It wouldn't do for my hands to shake, or for my heart to be pumping so hard that the blood came too fast to stop. No, I could wait a day. I would sleep and come back at first light when the sun was at the back of the house and its rays through the kitchen window would serve to illuminate my work.

Then I see myself in the full-length mirror that leans dusty against the wall. I see the roundness in my cheeks, my eyes set deep above them. Beneath the hem of my t-shirt, once black, now stained and faded to gray. A wide band of pale flesh falls heavy over my sweatpants. I touch the spot, and it yields beneath my fingers. It must be now, I think, before I lose my nerve. I'll do it now or risk never doing it at all.

I'd rehearsed it in my head a hundred times and more. The moves I could make from memory. I fill the wide bowl with the flowers on the rim, and let the tap run a bit first to make sure it didn't come out too cold. I place it on the table next to the smaller blue bowl, empty now, but not for long. No, not for long.

The rest had already been laid out through careful practice. The tongs from the drawer of kitchen tools. An unused sponge I'd found hidden beneath the sink. Spools of black thread from Mama's sewing bag. I sit in my chair and make sure I can reach them all. I needn't have bothered, but still I make the moves one last time, my hand lingering on the blue and white box that I only now feel ready to open.

I draw out one of the long bundles inside and free it from its plastic wrapper. Its edges glint and glitter in the dusty beam of light from the window. I want to test it, but I know that it's sharp, so sharp, as sharp as I will ever need. Surgical steel delivered to my doorstep, each scalpel pre-sterilized and individually wrapped, every one a tiny miracle. Now that I had one in my hand I wondered how it had ever taken me so long to begin.

I frown at the stack of folded paper napkins. I'd wanted cloth but couldn't bear to sully mama's tea-towels. I wonder, not for the first time, whether I'll have enough, whether once I start cutting there will be too much to keep up with and the plastic trash bag I've draped over the back of the chair will get too full. I'd been through it over and over again inside my head, accounted for every last possibility, every way in which this could go wrong. What if there was something I'd failed to consider? What if, once I started, something went wrong that I could not fix?

I shake my head. I'd come too far to let myself become derailed by doubt. I strip off my t-shirt and wiggle my sweatpants down to the floor. I watch my stomach in the dusty mirror and follow how it gives and rolls beneath my fingers. Baby fat was what mama had always called it, and I'd try to twist away as she'd giggled and pinched, hard enough to leave marks. Subcutaneous, was what it was, and that one word made all the difference. If it had been the kind that wound its way beneath the muscle, around the liver and intestines, then there'd be nothing to be done for it. This fat was just below the skin, so close that I can imagine the feel of it against my bare fingers. Subcutaneous fat would be easy, so easy that it still amazes me that I took so long to realize just what I could do about it.

Not that I hadn't tried all the other ways first. I'd done my jumping jacks in the front room where the papers weren't so high, mama watching doubtfully from her chair in the corner as I huffed and puffed my way through push-ups and crunches. "I don't know what you're bothering for," Mama would say, her chair creaking as it rocked. "Ain't gonna make a bit of difference 'cept to make the whole house smell like a locker room!"

She was right, of course. In my heart I knew as much before I even started, and lest I forget she was always there, always, to remind me with her proddings and her biting scorn. I had no say in the food that came into our little house. I began eating less, but new snacks in bright-colored packages would find themselves arrayed near my place at the table. When I resisted, she took to eating them in front of me, sighing with pleasure at every bite until I could do nothing else but give in. I'd try to skip meals, but the meals would always be waiting for me. "Don't waste what the Lord has given," Mama would say, as if the Lord worked in a factory packing microwave dinners in flat little boxes. But this new plan, I can feel the certainty of it working with every anticipating beat of my heart. Best of all, Mama won't be here to get in my way.

I spread on the numbing cream, and almost forget to use the latex gloves. I'd done that once before, when I was helping mama with her sores, and it had left the tips of my fingers feeling like blunted, alien things. I force myself to slow down. I work the cream in deep, feeling its cold on my skin and then feeling nothing at all. The place where I'll cut is small, just to the right of my belly button, but I use more than I'll need anyway. It will be a small job. A pound, not more than two.

There's no pain, and just a little blood. The scalpel draws itself through my skin like a shark's fin cutting through the waves, and in an instant my body has a new opening. Three inches long, I can barely see it but for the little beads of red that well up along its length like tiny rubies. Despite my efforts, the cut is not completely straight. It curves away, toward the waistband of my underwear. I can almost imagine that it is smiling at me.

I pinch at its edges, forcing it open like a coin purse. The blood comes quicker now, and I reach for a paper towel to wipe it away. At last I can see my prize, a field of glistening yellow-gray just beyond the wound. I probe it with my finger, and it yields beneath my touch like molded gelatin. Now that I'm so close it seems like such a simple thing to rid myself of it, to reach in with my fingers and pull it out of me in great, heaping handfuls. But I began with a plan and I will follow that plan. It would not do to be careless, not with my goal close enough now that I can literally touch it.

Again I take up the scalpel, and again I cut, deeper this time. I feel the bite of the blade as it moves, but not enough to make me stop. The flow of blood has slowed to a trickle. I work slowly, describing a little circle no bigger than my thumbnail, waiting for a sharper pain, a more dangerous pain to tell me I've gone too far. But that pain never comes, and after a moment the little circle tugs free.

I hold it between thumb and blade, and bring it into the light. It is yellow and streaked with blood, and it wobbles as it moves. At once I am struck by how strange it is, this part of myself, once hidden, now naked and visible. It glistens like some parasitic grub, rendered harmless in the work of moments. I drop it in the little bowl. The needle on the scale twitches but does not move. One pound, perhaps two, and there is so much work left to do.

I swish the scalpel clean in the bowl of water. I work faster now, gaining confidence by the moment. The scalpel guides my hand as it describes a far larger circle than the last. Again I pull forth a jiggling mass and deposit it in the bowl upon the scale. The needle moves again, but it stays this time. I hear mama's mocking voice, but it is distant and faint and I know that it is not real.

Blood trickles from the wound in a steady stream, but I pay it no mind as I apply the blade again. It moves like a skater on ice, and I remind myself to slow down lest I cut too deep and nick something vital. But I have cut down to the full depth of the blade, and still I have only begun.

The blade glides, and then the blade stops. I try to draw it along but it will not move. It is as if it has become caught against something hard and unyielding, and my mind begins to panic as it races to understand what it might be. I have not cut so deep as to touch muscle or bone. Could it be that I missed something in my preparations, some vital blood vessel or length of connective tissue?

I have no time to attempt an answer. The blade twitches and jerks in my hand and sinks deep into the yellow-gray fat. It is only when the handle is half-submerged in the spongy mass that I am able to grasp it enough to make it stop. I pull, but it will not come. Something has taken hold of the scalpel. I can feel it countering my efforts as I try to pull the blade free. The handle slips against my bloody fingers, and I hold on with both hands to keep it from sinking away entirely. Whatever it is that fights me seems to match me strength for strength, and it takes everything I have just to keep my grip. The scalpel sinks deeper, and I fear that I have lost, until at once something gives way with a snap.

I sit in the chair, the scalpel in my fist. The sound of my racing heart pounds in my ears, beating in time to the lazy pulse of the blood that wells up from the hole in my body where I pulled the thing free. It beads against the edge of the cut in my skin and rolls down the great curve of my belly. My eyes go wide as I see the scalpel, streaked in red, and my throat begins to tighten.

The blade is broken, a new blunt edge in place of sharpened steel. The tip of it is missing.

I try to sleep, but sleep won't come. There's a fly in the room and it has trapped itself between the window and the curtain. I lie in the empty bed and stare at the ceiling, listening to the sound it makes as it throws itself against the glass. Buzz-click. Buzz-click. Buzz-click.

The cut in my stomach is sore and its edges sting when I touch them. I want to use more of the numbing cream but it burns in the raw opening when I try to put it on. The thread from Mama's sewing kit is strong, and the stitches are holding despite the shaking hand that made them. They pull at my skin as I shift my weight. My stomach growls but I will not eat.

I stare at the ceiling and try not to think of the broken tip of the scalpel. It is small, no bigger than the nail on my little finger, but it is sharp and it is still inside me. In those moments when the fly stops buzzing I can feel it working beneath the wound, gliding by millimeters through the same slick and yielding tissue that I'd touched with my own hands just hours before.

It will have to come out. I am tired and my thoughts are addled by hunger and pain, but I know this much above all else. And yet, the thought of taking up another scalpel from the little blue and white box sends a cold tingle of dread down my spine. It isn't fear of the cutting. No, it is the memory of the blade being tugged from my hand by something strong enough to break sharpened steel.

The fly strikes the window and I feel the thing inside me turn, dragging the little shard with it. How long has it been there, lurking beneath the surface of my skin? Is it some kind of parasite, like the worms in third-world countries that burrow in so deep that they have to be pried out with a stick? Was it lurking in something I ate, some spoiled bit of meat, or vegetables from a dented can? Or has it always been a part of me, lying in wait, biding its time until the right moment to assert itself, a moment I provided when I touched the scalpel to my skin?

There's a sag in the mattress in the spot where Mama used to sleep, where the slats beneath it are cracked and bowed. I find myself sliding toward it. My stomach churns. I know that I should get up. I know that I should walk past the cellar door into the kitchen and find myself some food. I fight to keep my place and I remember Mama, the way she would watch me when I passed the boxes of cakes she'd left out on the table, her eyes almost daring me. The thing inside me writhes at the thought. To feed myself means feeding it as well, and that I will not do.

———◦———

I wake to the light of midday and the chill of sweat drying against my skin. The fly has stopped buzzing, though whether it has finally died or just moved on, I do not know. I am slow to move, my senses groggy. What little sleep I found was fitful and plagued by dark dreams. I find the stitches with my fingertips, if only to assure myself that it was real, that I had not dreamed it all. My jaw tightens as I touch them. The wound aches, and the skin around it is warm.

With effort, I pry myself from the bed and make my way to the bathroom. The vast curve of my stomach aches as if someone had spent the night using it as a punching bag, but it is still. The thing inside it is at rest. Perhaps, like the fly, it too has died. Perhaps, if I'm patient, I can find where it has hidden the bit of the scalpel blade and at last remove it, along with the corpse of whatever it was that stole it from me, be it worm or larva or something I have not yet imagined.

It is a calming thought, but even as it occurs to me, it doesn't seem credible. The thing is still inside me. I can sense it there, waiting. If I have any doubt of that, it is gone the instant I turn on the bathroom light.

I see myself reflected in the dirty mirror, a sticky smear of blood drying into my underwear. The great, pale curve of my belly sags over the waistband. There, beneath the cavern of my navel, lies a series of sharp slashes, narrow bruises, purple edged with red. Together they form a single word, unmistakable, even backward in the spattered glass:

FEED

I stagger back against the doorframe. Knees that were never strong threaten to buckle and send me crashing to the floor. I do not let them. The thing that wrote the word is still inside me and I will not show it weakness. I feel it turn within me, a lazy flip, as if to punctuate the word, to let me know that it is there, waiting. But I will not, must not, obey. To feed it I must feed myself, and this I cannot do.

The thought barely has time to solidify in my mind before I feel the thing move again. There is no leisurely turn this time as it drives with force and intention deep into the center of my stomach. At its head, the broken bit of scalpel blazes a path of white-hot pain, tearing through the yielding flesh as it bores deeper and deeper.

The pain doubles me over, and though I cannot bring myself to speak, my mind screams over and over that I will concede, that I will do whatever it asks if only it will stop and give me a moment to breathe. But it does not relent, and I feel the sharpened steel edging closer to muscle and bone.

I stagger into the hall, groping wildly, pulling myself along the walls. My hand finds the knob on the cellar door. It turns beneath my fingers but I will not allow it to open, not even now. The metal shard drives once more, then slows as if it has met some new resistance. I feel its point against the muscle above my hip, turning my movements against me. Every step is a fiery, breathless stab.

At last I reach the pantry door. The pain retreats as I swing it aside. Sweat cools on my forehead and in the shallow folds of my skin. I scan the rows of soups, of canned corn and green beans, but I know they will not do. As if in confirmation, the little shard cuts again, not inward this time, but upward. It is a gentle, almost friendly prod, and I raise my eyes along with its motion. There, on the top shelf, are the boxes that Mama would stack on the table to taunt me, yellow cakes with white frosting, little rolls of chocolate wrapped in plastic, heavy sugar robed in foil.

I think of the delivery man, of the muscles in his calf, hard and lean beneath his skin. I think of walking to the corner in the sunlight, and I begin to cry. Please, I beg, not knowing what it is I'm pleading with. I don't want it. Please, just leave me alone. I hold my breath, and all is quiet for an instant. Then the metal turns inside me, and I know I've been given my answer.

The blade retreats again as I reach up and take one of the boxes from the shelf. It is already open, and as I pull out one of the plastic-wrapped bundles it crinkles pleasantly between my fingers. The thing inside me is quiet now, anticipating. The wrapping parts so easily, and as the smell of its contents hits me I begin to salivate in spite of myself. With tears on my lips I bring it to my mouth and take a bite.

It is good. It is so, very good.

⚬

I watch the delivery man through the gap in the curtains. The box he carries is large enough that he needs both hands to hold it, but he maneuvers it with ease. I can see the muscles of his arms flex as he places it on the porch. I want to wait until nightfall before I open the door to bring the box inside, but I know the thing inside me will not let me. I watch the man walk back down the driveway and climb into his truck. It allows me that much, at least. Then the awful prodding begins, and I know that I can keep it waiting no longer.

I move so much slower now. It takes me full minutes to negotiate the narrow path to the door. My legs are swollen and my knees hurt. My arms are heavy. There are stretch marks on my stomach, like growth rings on a tree trunk. I brush against the stacks of magazines, of overstuffed plastic grocery bags as I pass. I hear them fall behind me, but I do not stop to pick them up.

I hurry to wrestle the box inside, rocking it on its corners, dragging it toward the door. It is heavier than the delivery man's movements had led me to believe, and I look around to make sure there's no one to witness my struggle. The sunlight reflects off my pale cheeks and hurts my eyes. With one last kick, I heave it inside. I am out of breath, and as I close the door behind me, I lean against it for support.

My keeper flips and I am moving again, dragging the box to the kitchen. The pantry is nearly empty now. I have eaten everything inside it, from the cakes in their little wrappers to the sauces in their glass jars. There is more in the cellar. I recall rows of peaches and pears in rusting cans, but I will not go down there, not even at the prodding of the metal shard. My keeper knows this, I think, and it does not ask it of me.

A stack of empty cans clatters to the floor as I pry the box open, and a cloud of flies buzzes into the air. I bat them away as I sort the box's contents and stack them on the table. I push the scale and the bowls aside. The water has long since dried, and the little lump of flesh that I pried from myself is mummified and maggoty.

I tear open a bag of potato chips. I've never liked them. They are too salty and they give me headaches, but I eat them anyway. My keeper prefers them, and makes its inclinations known by the words it raises on my skin. SALT. SUGUR. MORE. The broken blade has traveled beyond my stomach, gliding through fatty pathways into my chest, my thighs, making my whole body its canvass. The spellings are often wrong and the letters are sometimes backwards, but they are enough, and I obey.

That earliest word is faded now, barely readable against a field of purple and yellow. My cut strains at its stitches, the skin around it red and angry. I wipe the grease from my hand on my sweatpants and try to touch it. It is hot, and it aches beneath my fingers.

I pull more chips from the bag and crunch them slowly. Beneath my skin, the blade is busy. It moves in lazy circles, but it moves with a purpose. I swallow hard. The salt burns my throat even as hot tears burn my cheeks. I think, and not for the first time, of stuffing my mouth, of using my fingers to push the half-chewed mass down my windpipe. My keeper pauses its labors, as if daring me. I only thrust my hand back into the bag. The work inside me begins again. I close my eyes, and when I do, I can almost see Mama smirking back at me.

Days flow past. I can no longer tell where one ends and another begins. Has it been weeks? A month? All time is measured in the space between feedings, when I only stop because my stomach has stretched near to breaking. My body has become a factory. Materials go in. Waste comes out. The product grows beneath my skin, new layers of yellow-gray flesh, pliable and ever expanding. I wonder sometimes at what it all must look like, but I will never know. I have broken every mirror in the house.

I have given up all hope of sleep. The broken blade is at work all night now, always moving, always cutting. It makes its way across my chest and into my arms, through my groin and around my thighs. I lie awake and watch as its movements make ripples in my new flesh and raise new bruises on my skin. Sometimes when it cuts I can feel something inside me snap, like the breaking of a guitar string. It cuts and cuts and does not stop, not even when I scream.

More than once I have thought to make an end of it. I have taken a fresh scalpel from its wrapper and laid it against the pulsing artery at the side of my neck. I pressed the point into my skin, but I could not drive it home. My arm belonged to my keeper now, and it would not move until I let the knife fall from my fingers. At least, that is how I remember it. My thoughts are jumbled and plagued by fever, and I am no longer certain of what is real.

The flies in the house are thick now. They light on my wound as I lay sweating in the night. I bat them away but they always return, drawn by the smell and the steady dribble of gray-green that oozes from the cut. It hurts too much to touch it now, so I do my best not to. It hurts too much to move at all, so I only move when I have to, when it is required of me.

It is required of me now. My keeper urges me to stand, and so we stand. I am dizzy and I stumble, but I allow myself a little smile because I know at last that I have nothing more to give.

The pantry is bare. We stagger to it and throw the door aside, touching the shelves one by one, but they are all empty. The delivery man will not come when there is no money left to pay the bills. I cannot feed my keeper when there is no food left to eat.

This, then, will be my triumph. I could not cut it out, but now, at last, I will starve it out. I will lay in my bed, and as my hunger consumes me the organs of my body will consume the very layers of flesh my keeper has compelled me to build. I will waste away, and as I do my keeper, too, will waste, denied the very fuel it requires to keep the blade moving inside me, denied the outcome of whatever strange purpose it has set for itself.

From the corner of my eye I glance at the scalpel lying on the kitchen floor. I think to carry it with me, to keep it in my hand until the time, maybe days from now, maybe weeks, when my keeper will no longer be strong enough to stop me. When it can no longer fight, I will press the blade to my throat and end us both. A final act of defiance. A final assertion of myself. I try to take the scalpel but it will not let me. I try to return to the bed, but my keeper has other plans.

We turn toward the hallway. A strangled cry of panic rises from my mouth, for I know exactly where it means to go. Somehow it has read my secret thoughts and it knows about the jars and the cans stacked away in the cellar. I fight every step, but I fight in vain. It is too strong, and if it has its way it will grow stronger still.

We pause before the cellar door. I feel my keeper retreat, inviting me, daring me, to do the next part on my own. I place my hand upon the knob. I haven't touched it in months, not since Mama died. Even now, I can feel her mocking me, waiting for me to act, knowing that I am powerless not to.

I turn the knob and push the door aside. It gives way with a faint creak, and a cloud of flies rises up to meet me. I pull the chain to turn on the light, but see nothing because my eyes are closed. My keeper gives an encouraging flutter and I breathe deep in spite of the smell.

Mama is there at the base of the stairs. She lies on the concrete amid the shards of the wooden handrail, and she's wearing a floral-patterned dress that I remember from as far back as my childhood. She's wasted away inside it, and it covers what is left of her like a shroud. Her cheeks are sunken and the flies have taken her eyes, but still she looks up at me, her head cocked sideways on her broken neck, accusing. A trail of blood, dried and sticky, leads away to the drain in the floor. She is blocking the way, and we will have to step over her when we get to the bottom. I do not want to get that close to her.

My keeper has retreated. Is it in sympathy? Has it sensed that this new thing it asks of me is too much, and is it giving me the space to do it alone? I look down into the darkness, knowing that I would as soon fling myself down the narrow stairs as lumber my way to the bottom. It would be so easy, the slightest of movements, slighter still than the push at Mama's back that sent her pinwheeling down there a lifetime ago. My keeper senses the thought and coils against it. And yet, I can move, and my movements are still my own.

I place an eager foot on the stair. My great weight tilts forward and the wood beneath me creaks in protest. My keeper writhes and slithers like an eel and I can sense its fear, for we both know that what I have just set in motion cannot be stopped. Gravity takes me, and for an instant I feel myself floating in air, as if weightless. My keeper gives a self-satisfied flip, and I realize that it is not fear that I sense, but anticipation.

It is too late to stop myself. My feet drag and I tumble down and down. My arm snaps. I hear it but I do not feel it. My body quakes around me as I cartwheel, upside-down and rightside-up, and on and on until at last I crash to a stop. I cannot move. My keeper is still, and the last thing I am aware of before the world goes dark is that I have fallen next to Mama, and her hand is in my own. Try as I might, I cannot hold it.

<hr />

The cellar floor is hard and cold, pitted concrete and the dust of ages. Inch by inch I gather myself, pulling, finding new energy with every labored move. My spine is broken, but I no longer feel it. The indignity and the pain of these past weeks has faded away to nothing. I reach for the memory, but it bursts and scatters like a cloud of flies.

My stitches have split. The cut is so much longer now. It stretches to my chest and curves back down past my groin and into my thigh. The skin hangs loose and wide, like the cover of an old book, the void beyond it deep and red. My eyes are open and they are turned up toward the light. I look back at them and I see them, but I do not know how.

The tip of the broken scalpel clatters to the floor. The last cuts have been made, and like all good tools I can lay it aside, satisfied that its work is done. Like the moth, I have emerged from my chrysalis, born anew and ready to fly. I stare at the limp and flabby thing as I lurch away. It seems small, too small to have ever contained me. I see the dried and eyeless thing in the floral dress, and I wonder how it ever had any power over me.

I am almost to the floor drain now. The distant, older part of my mind tells me that all I need do is follow it, and it will take me away from this place. I reach out beyond the opening, tendrils thin and probing, and I know that it is true. I seep past the grating, and as I do, a thought buzzes across my consciousness, the memory of a muscled calf, of a man standing in the sunlight. I find water, and as I begin to float along its gentle current I push the thought away. I no longer need the sunlight, and as the pipes guide me beyond the street corner and on beneath the next and the next, I feel something stir within me. It is a hunger, and I follow it where it leads me, ready at last to feed.

Origin Story

"If you had a super power, what would it be?"

"You mean, what would my power be if I could pick for myself? Or what would my power be if I was a character in a comic book and I ended up with a power that fit me as a person?"

A moment's pause, and then, "I hadn't really thought about it that way, but let's do the second."

Phil shrugged. "Well, knowing my luck, it would be something completely useless. We're nowhere near an ocean, so it'd probably be something to do with fish. Talk to them, summon them, make them do stuff. It may not seem like much, but if someone ever committed a crime in a pet store or an aquarium, I'd be your guy."

Darryl didn't look up from the issue spread out on the counter in front of him. "I guess that would make you The Crayfish."

Phil. Phillip Cray. The Crayfish. Phil stared past the panels in his own book and realized that he'd probably just earned a nickname that would last him the rest of his life.

"What about you?" he asked.

Darryl answered immediately, as if it was something he kept on the tip of his tongue at all times, ready at an instant's notice. "I'd have the ability to compress matter, to make it so small that it could pass through quantum holes in space-time and travel instantaneously from one point in space to another."

"Oh, is that all?"

"It's enough."

"And is this the power that you'd pick or the power that fits your character?"

Darryl didn't answer. If it was because he was too lost in the world of his comic book or because he'd just lost interest in the conversation, Phil couldn't tell. Darryl was like that, so Phil had learned. He'd latch on to whatever hot-button geek-issue crossed his mind, pursue it, debate it and argue it into a corner until it no longer suited him. Then he'd pretend he'd never brought it up in the first place, especially if he found himself on the losing end. Phil didn't complain, though, since Darryl was the one who signed the checks that kept him behind the counter of Fantasy Flight Comix and well away from the certain horror of The Respectable Job. Besides, Darryl was mostly an okay guy. Mostly.

It went on like that for most of the day, Phil on his side of the counter, Darryl on his. They made almost perfect counterpoints to each other, Darryl with his girth, his close-cropped hair and glasses, Phil with his stringbean physique and grunge-rock scruffiness.

It was a Thursday, which made it a slow day. All the serious collectors had come the day before, when the new issues came in. Thursday customers, what few there were, were tourists, and were greeted with indifference bordering on scorn. As they browsed the racks there was an almost funereal, library-patron way about them, as if they knew that they had entered some-place holy, that they were treading somewhere they could never truly belong. Darryl and Phil took their money all the same, rarely making eye contact, reveling silently in their self-ascribed superiority.

It was late in the afternoon, after the single-issue sales and the countless others who left empty-handed, before Darryl spoke again. He shifted his weight back on his stool and turned to Phil, his brow furrowed in thought.

"This fish power of yours. How did you get it?"

"You mean the cosmic event that forever transformed mild-mannered Phillip Cray into The Crayfish, unstoppable force for justice?" Better to own the nickname now. Maybe Darryl would see it didn't get to him, and he'd lose interest in that, too.

"The very same."

"Hypothetically?"

"Hypothetically."

Phil thought it over, suddenly taking pleasure in the game. He hit upon the answer and grinned. "Mobsters."

"Mobsters?"

"I saw too much, and they had to get rid of me. So they tie me up, throw me in the trunk of a car and drive me to the pier. They hook weights to me, they throw me in, and I drown. Then a shark comes by. Maybe he's looking for food. Maybe he's sent by the sea gods to help me out. Anyway, his fin grazes one of my ropes and cuts it. So, I float free and as the tide comes in, I get caught in a school of fish that pushes me up on shore. That's when, suddenly, I start to breathe again. And I can talk to fish. Voila! The Crayfish is born!"

"That's already been done a hundred times."

"But not with fish."

"Sure it has. I could name at least three."

"Well, now you can name four."

Darryl shrugged and went back to his book. "I thought you said you didn't live near water."

"All right, smart guy. You think you can do better?"

"Hm?"

"All that matter shrinking whosamawhatsit."

"Compressing."

"Compressing. Whatever. How do you come by that little gem?"

Darryl closed his book and raised his head, a gesture of seriousness and respect-for-topic that Phil had seen only once before. "I don't know. Maybe it was one of those things where I always had it and it just took this long to develop. Maybe it's a cosmic event and it lets loose powers in other people, too. Maybe it's something that just happens. One day you're normal and the next day... boom."

As he spoke, there was a faraway look in his eyes, an earnestness that seemed to belie the disdain and apathy that was as much a part of who he was as his sweat-ringed t-shirts.

"Those have all been done, too."

"Yeah, but not like this." He looked up at the clock and allowed himself a little grin. "It's quarter 'till. Let's lock up early. I've got something to show you."

Five minutes later, they were out in the crisp, fall air and well into the six-block hike from the store to Darryl's place. The big man moved with quick, determined steps. His head was down and forward, as if he meant to stay ahead of his own bulk, as if gravity itself was propelling him along. Phil followed at a stutter-step, almost having to trot to keep up.

That phrase, "I've got something to show you," always preceded something wondrous. If not wondrous, then at least noteworthy, even if it was noteworthy only to Darryl. Phil wondered with a vague sense of anticipation what it would be this time. Perhaps some vintage action figure he found online. Maybe a bootleg episode of some long-forgotten sci-fi TV show. Doubtless, it was some artifact of significance, the latest addition to a vast collection, over which Darryl would beam like a proud parent. Whatever it was, he was in a hurry to get back to it.

Their path took them down a street where, up ahead, three lean, straggle-haired kids stood at the corner. One straddled a bike while the other two shoved at each other playfully, getting rid of pent-up energy. They were not quite teenagers, but carried themselves as if they were in a hurry to get there. Darryl lowered his head even more as he drew closer, and Phil could see that this wasn't the first time he had crossed their path.

One of the shovers noticed him first. He stopped shoving and made a show of trying to be casual as he elbowed the kid on the bike. The kid on the bike smiled and began to stare at Darryl as he lurched toward them. Before long, all three of them were staring, wicked little grins on each of their faces.

Those grins said it all, every insult that came to their minds, every name they could have called him, had called him, and would have called him if he had been alone. Phil and Darryl passed them, and as they did, Phil could hear the whispers, the muffled snickers that followed after them. He caught himself searching the ground, looking for a rock to throw, but banished the thought as soon as it came. There were better things ahead: all the wonders of Darryl's collection, new and old. Best of all was that look on Darryl's face, the awe and pride that cared nothing for the unspoken insults of little children.

<hr>

"There has to be a point to it." Darryl sorted through his keys, the metal frame of the screen door propped against his arm.

"A point to what?" Phil asked.

"The fish. Your power. There has to be a reason for it or it doesn't make sense."

"Why does there have to be a reason?"

The door popped open with a squeak and let out a breath of air, close and human, like old laundry. "Because without a reason, it's just a gift. A gift doesn't mean anything. It's just something you get."

"What's wrong with that?"

"Everything."

Darryl's living room was something that should have belonged to a man three times his age: a battered couch with yellowed doilies on the armrests, an old pull-chain lamp with a broken shade, a dusty carpet marked by matted clumps of cat hair. Amid it all were the boxes: tidy, age-worn bins full of magazines and papers, stacks of comic books well known and long forgotten. They'd been piled high and deep, with little trenches of bare floor left behind in case anyone should ever want to peruse them.

The place was so familiar to Phil that he was beyond giving the mess a second thought. But something was different today, and though he couldn't quite figure what it was, it caused his eyes to linger. The answer was there, almost close enough to grasp, but then Darryl spoke again.

"With a gift, you don't have to give anything back. But if there's a *reason* for the gift, then it becomes a mission. Suddenly you have a purpose in life. It's the power that gives you that purpose. Or, maybe you had the purpose all along but didn't know it until you received the power. Either way, there's a point to all of it."

Phil could see the excitement in the big man's face, the single-minded insistence in the way he was standing, in the set of his jaw. Phill's thoughts immediately shifted to the front door, to the number of steps, the number of seconds it would take for him to reach it and open it. The feeling came and went, replaced by a wave of shame.

"So," said Darryl, "what's the point of your power?"

"What's the point of yours?"

"That's the real question, isn't it?" His face registered the hint of a grin, a wistful, far away look. It was gone in a moment, replaced by his usual grim stoicism. "Come on," he said. "What I want to show you is right downstairs."

Again, that feeling of hesitation. Phil felt it sending tingles from the base of his neck up into his scalp. His feet felt heavy, getting ready to run. He might have done it, gone sprinting for the door and out into the street, had Darryl not reached for the door to the stairs and started down them, ahead of him.

If he had seen the doubt on Phil's face, he gave no sign. He just trundled down the wooden steps, boards creaking with age and strain as he made his way. If he had waited, insisted somehow that Phil go first, then there might have been cause to go running out the door. But Darryl had gone first, and that made him harmless. Still, Phil did not want the big man behind him.

Darryl stopped a few stairs down and turned back to face him. There was a look there that Phil had not seen before. It was more than the usual distant acceptance. This was something closer to friendship. "I trust you," he said. "You know that, right?"

At once, Phil realized that he might just be the only friend that Darryl had. He was a poor friend at that, one who barely tolerated Darryl's existence on most days, only taking an interest in his life when there was some new treasure to be seen. The shame came over him again, this time to stay. Darryl started down the stairs once more, and this time, Phil followed.

"The thing about having a power," Darryl said, "is that it lets you do stuff that you always wanted to do, but that you knew you couldn't because you weren't strong enough. But it's stuff you have to do, stuff you were born to do. The only thing you've been lacking all your life was the means."

They were almost to the bottom now. Phil could see the first few rows of Darryl's action figure collection, tiered displays like in a museum. He knew that there were more just like it around the corner, but suddenly, he didn't want to see around that corner. He didn't want to know what might be down there waiting for him.

"That's why it's so important that the power have a point to it," Darryl said. "If you weren't picked, if you weren't *chosen*, then you're just some jerk with a power. It doesn't mean a thing. You were just lucky enough to get something you don't deserve, and I refuse to believe that.

They were at the bottom of the stairs now. There was nothing unexpected there, nothing waiting, nothing out of place. Nothing, except Darryl's face. It shone with newfound pride, a sense of place that he had been looking his whole life to find.

Suddenly Phil was seeing him, the real Darryl, not the image of him he'd tried so hard to portray. He had lost weight, at least twenty pounds. Why had he not noticed that before now? All the signs were there: fresh fruit for snacks instead of candy bars, diet shakes instead of cheeseburgers. Darryl had hidden his transformation, subtle though it was, beneath a baggy t-shirt. But now Phil could see past the disguise.

"You already know what I'm going to tell you," said Darryl. Phil nodded.

Darryl smiled, this time with his entire face, more confident, more collected than ever before. "Good. I knew I got that much right. Come on. It's right around the corner."

He led the way past the toys, the posters, the obsessions of a lifetime. Beyond them was a wooden door frame covered with a black sheet, something Phil had seen many times but never given a single thought to.

"You see, if this had just been some sort of accident, if I had been walking down the street and gotten hit by radiation or toxic sludge or something, I could just call it dumb luck. But it just happened, right out of the blue, which means that somewhere out there, there's a plan for me. And if there was a plan, I knew that some day, I would find out what it was, and before that day came, I had to be ready."

He drew aside the curtain

Beyond it was a room, but more than just a room. It was lit only by the glow from three monitors, each large enough to dominate the space by itself, aligned one beside the other in a loose horseshoe. One was tuned to cable news, another to a weather station. The one in the middle was attached to a computer, and on it shone a map of the city, little areas marked out in red, others in blue. Before them was a desk doing double-duty as a workbench. Clusters of wiring and ambiguous electronics lay strewn between stacks of paper. At its edge, an old sewing machine with a yellowed plastic housing clung to a length of dark fabric: the beginnings of a costume.

Phil wondered at once how many first editions, how many rare treasures had been sacrificed on this altar before him. He wondered how much of Darryl himself had been in those books, those irreplaceable items that he held so dear. He wondered how much of himself Darryl had left behind.

Then he noticed the smell.

It came at him all at once, low and earthy, like meat left out to rot. The air seemed weighed down by it, and it made Phil's stomach want to heave its contents out onto the floor. He kept it in check, but only barely. If Darryl noticed his reaction, or if he even smelled it itself, he gave no sign.

"This is why I brought you here," Darryl said. "You're my friend, and that means one of two things. You know how this works as well as I do. You know how these things happen. You can tell me what all of this is for. You can help me find the purpose!"

His eyes were wide, and as he spoke, he seemed to get taller. There was pride in his voice, but those eyes betrayed his insecurity. He was watching Phil, waiting for him to speak. But Phil had no words. It was all too much, this place, the idea that someone he had known for years could— Then, at the edge of his vision, he saw something move.

It was in the deep shadows beyond the monitors. Phil's eyes were still adjusting to the darkness, but he could make out a deeper shadow at the edge of the floor, a crawlspace whose boundaries were lost in the distance. There, in the midst of that space, two glowing pinpoints stared out at him.

Then Phil realized all at once what had been missing upstairs, what he should have known right away. If he had seen it then he would never have come to the basement, that much he was sure of now. There should have been at least five of them underfoot, weaving their way among his legs, tripping him as he walked. But the cats hadn't been there. Phil should have seen that, and ran.

"The power's kind of tricky," Darryl said. "I haven't quite gotten the hang of it, but I will. It's all about precision, really. If you want to move something, you have to squish it down really small. The hard part is figuring out how to make it come back right."

The thing in the crawlspace was edging toward them now. Phil could just make out the whiskers jutting from its face. Something about the movement of it was all wrong. It seemed to lurch forward, hesitating as if some great weight was holding it back. Phil stared, not wanting to look, but unable to turn away. A sound came from deep within the thing's throat, something between a wet gurgle and a purr. It made heavy scraping sounds as it dragged itself across the gravel floor, halting with pain at every step.

"She was my first try," Darryl said. "I managed to move her almost four feet, but she came back, well... The others didn't do as well. They're back there if you want me to show you."

"Darryl, this is—"

"I know. It's amazing. I tried making it work on other stuff, like a chair, an ashtray. But I couldn't do it. It needs a heartbeat. It needs a pulse."

"It's horrible."

"That's what I thought at first, too. It's too limited. I could go through hundreds, even thousands of tries before I figured out how to get it right. That's why I made this place. This city's a mess, Phil. Drug dealers, thieves, prostitutes... the dregs of society. This place would be better off without them."

Phil looked at the computer screen again, at the map with the spots marked in blue. All the worst neighborhoods. All the places where Darryl should have been afraid to go.

"I've been there, Phil. I've gone at night to the places that most people wouldn't visit in the daylight. I've been close, so close that it would have been easy. All I would have had to do was reach out with my hand and they'd be gone, just like that. But I waited, Phil. I waited for you."

The thing in the crawlspace let out a low grunt, and Phil thought he could see something bubble and pop loose from its side.

"That's why I brought you here. You've read the stories the same as me. You know there's always someone close, someone to help figure out what it all means, what it's all for."

"Darryl, you can't—"

"I can! But I can't do it alone. There's so many choices, so many wrongs to right. They used to make fun of me. They belittled me all my life, but they wouldn't have if they had known. They would have been afraid. Not me! Them! But there's so many! And so many just like them! How do I know where to start?"

There was a wildness about him now, excitement mixed with a lifetime of fear. Yet, beneath it was a kind of confidence, a sense that that everything he said made perfect sense, that the confirmation he was looking for was almost within his grasp.

"Start?" Phil said. "You have to *stop*!"

The confidence drained down the corners of Darryl's mouth. "But, this is what I've been waiting for all my life."

"No, it's not, Darryl. I don't know what happened to you, but this isn't a comic book. It's not right. We have to call the police, get you to a doctor or—"

Phil stopped. Darryl's face had changed. Wild excitement was replaced with stark disappointment, fear with sadness. And beneath it all was a sense of grim determination. "Oh," he said. "It's the other way, then." As Darryl took a step forward, Phil realized what he had done.

"No, Darryl, don't."

"I wanted you there, Phil, I wanted you to see it happen. Now I'll have to do it alone." Another step forward, a fist clenched in the darkness.

"Darryl, please."

"I guess I was wrong, Phil. At least this way you'll still be helping me, even if it is for only a minute."

"This isn't what heroes do."

The fist opened into a hand, and in the palm, something began to swirl, like oil on a moonlit lake.

"Who said anything about being a hero?"

The hand came up. It gave off a blue glow that lit the room, and Darryl held it stiff-armed in front of him. Phil knew he couldn't run, that there wasn't enough room, enough time. The hand inched closer, and he closed his eyes.

Then Darryl fell.

Phil heard the sharp crack of skull on concrete, the ragged gasps of fading breath. It was only when that breath stopped that he finally opened his eyes. Darryl's eyes were open, too, his last look one of surprise, perhaps even wonder. Where his foot had slipped, something new and wet was still flopping.

The thing in the crawlspace gathered itself and lurched out into the open. It found the burst flesh at the spot where it had been pierced by Darryl's boot heel, and began to feed.

Phil backed away, not wanting to watch, not wanting to stay in that place one second more. As he turned for the stairs, the last thing he saw was the beast's ruined face, the fish still flopping in its jaws, retreating into the dark.

Poppy

It's stupid, I know. I mean, I hear myself. I know how I sound. And I see the way you're looking at me. I remember that look. It's the same look you had, you know, *back then*. When things were bad. I bet you're probably thinking you dodged a bullet, right? Broke up with the crazy bitch just in time, got out of there before she went full-tilt bonkers and started raving like a lunatic in the middle of the coffee shop.

Wait. That's not fair. Could you just... sit? Please.

I'm sorry. I mean, I know you didn't have to come. You didn't even have to answer the phone, not after everything I did. And I wouldn't have blamed you one bit if you'd just blocked my number and never had anything to do with me again. But you picked up. I was so afraid that you wouldn't, but I didn't know who else to call. I don't have anyone else. No one who wouldn't immediately think I'm completely out of my mind, at least. And you're here. A part of me didn't think that I'd ever see you again, but here you are, and I...

I'm sorry. I'm completely screwing this up, aren't I? I'm sorry. I'm saying that a lot, I know. I mean it, though. I do.

Okay. Deep breaths. I'm just going to start at the start because I don't know any other way to keep it all straight in my head. I just need you to listen. And you *will* listen, right? I know I don't really have the right to ask you for that, but I need you to listen.

And you don't have to believe me, okay. I mean, I probably wouldn't even believe me. I'm not even sure that *I* believe me right now, like my mind just can't deal again and it's playing all these tricks on me just to keep me from going all the way nuts. But it's not that, not this time. And I need someone to listen to me. Someone I trust, I mean. And I need to tell it now. It won't make any sense later unless I tell it now.

So, yeah, there's this girl. And you can wipe that smirk off your face right now. It wasn't like that. I'm talking about the store here. She's an employee. Hired her three months ago when Lyden quit. You remember Lyden, right? Shaved head. Eyebrow ring. Arms sleeved up with tattoos so dark that you'd swear he was just wearing another shirt? Anyway, he got poached by the game store across from the food court. Can't hold it against him, though. Half the work and probably better pay, ripping kids off, paying pennies for used games and turning them around at ten times the price. Didn't even give notice, the little shit. Just up and left one day and never clocked back in.

Anyway, I put a sign up on the door and two days later she walks in with the thing in her hand like she already knows I'm going to give her the job. And I could tell just looking at her that I was going to give her the job. She was wearing a black dress, all poofy black lace and black stockings up just above her knees. Her hair was black too, of course, and cut down to a little bob that looked rough enough that she'd probably done it herself. She had a silver stud in her nose and a pair of flirty little ankh earrings like she was some Neil Gaiman superfan. She had pale skin, so pale that you'd swear it would chip if you brushed up against her too hard.

But for all that darkness, it was like she brought the sun into the store with her. She had this... energy—this life—around her. It was like a magnet. I knew all I had to do was have her stock shelves up at the front of the store and all the slouchy little goths and skater punks would start streaming in just for the chance to avoid making eye contact with her. Not that any of them ever spend money, no. But a little foot traffic can turn into a lot of foot traffic once people see that you're starting to get busy, that there's a reason to come inside, right? And she was reason enough all on her own. She looked like Lydia from Beetlejuice, or maybe that girl from Death Note. Goth, but cute about it, so cute you just wanted to pick her up and put her in your pocket.

And yes, I guess I was a little smitten, too. I have a type. I know this. Hell, you *were* that type, back when we first met. That hot little undercut hairdo you had? And all that eyeliner! You remember that little matador jacket you used to wear? How you put it around my shoulders that first night, when you saw that I was cold? Well, I remember, anyway. I thought about that jacket a lot, you know, when I was away. It kept me going, in a lot of ways. I don't think I ever told you that, but it did.

Anyway, it was never like that with Poppy. That was her name. Poppy. She never looked at me that way, not the way you used to. And why would she, now that I'm on the wrong side of thirty and the cutest thing in my wardrobe is a baggy t-shirt that probably still has food stains on it? Don't roll your eyes like that. It's true, and I'm okay with it. At least I'm better than I was, you know, *before*. But no, I didn't want to get with her. She was tiny, five foot nothing and ninety pounds at the most, and from the moment I saw her, it was like I wanted to protect her. She had that air about her, like she might break at any second, and I probably would have done anything to keep it from happening. After a while, I felt responsible for her, like a big sister. And I suppose that's what she was to me. The little sister I never had.

Was. I said *was* just now. Jesus, I'd hoped this would be easier. Are you sure you still want to hear it?

Okay.

I was right about the foot traffic, though. And it wasn't just the horny teenagers, though we certainly saw our fair share of those. It was little old ladies, and big fat guys in trucker hats, and college kids who wouldn't have been caught dead in the place before she showed up. She'd wave at people through the big front window while she was dressing out the mannequins. Whoever it was—it didn't matter—they'd wave back and be-fore you know it, they'd be inside, looking kind of dazed and squinting into the glass cabinet where we keep all the bongs locked up. You know the one. Right next to the register with the little sign that says "For Tobacco Use Only." Not like it ever fooled anybody.

And it wasn't like Poppy was one of those tedious extroverts. You know the ones: taking perfect selfies for Instagram all the time, never stop bragging about how damn wonderful everything is. No, that wasn't Poppy at all. She was quiet. Not exactly shy, but more *reserved*, I guess. Like there was something on her mind that you just knew she was never going to tell you about. Maybe it was that, that little bit of mystery that she had about her. Whatever it was, when she was around, people couldn't help but pay attention. She was compelling. They felt it. I felt it. We all felt it. Right away, she became the center of the place, the beating heart that I never knew it was missing. I probably could have gone the rest of my life without missing it, either, but now... No matter how I try to fill that space again, it just feels...empty.

I wish I could say we became friends, but it was never like that, either. I've never been much good at that anyway. You know this, probably better than most. No, I was the boss and she was the employee, and that's as close as we got. And she was pretty good, as employees went. Most of these kids today—yeah, I sound like an old grandma. Deal with it—but most of them just clock in and take up space until it's time for them to clock out again. You have to spell things out and point them in the direction you want them to go like they're toddlers, and god forbid you don't praise them enough for doing the bare minimum. But Poppy, you could tell her once and that was it. Most times I didn't even have to tell her at all. She kept the earrings stocked, kept the counters clean, took to the credit card app like she'd been doing it her whole life. I never asked her where she worked before she got there. She didn't bring references or even a resume. Maybe I should have checked into her more, took some time before I said "sure, come on board." I don't know. I doubt it would have changed anything.

But I can't tell you about Poppy without telling you about the mannequins, too. I guess that's the part of all this that I've been avoiding. If I don't tell you now, I'm just going to keep stalling all night. I keep trying to figure out how to say it all so it makes sense. But it doesn't make sense. Maybe it'll never make sense. But you're still here. I haven't run you off yet. Not again, anyway. Will you stay while I tell you the rest? Once I start, I don't know if I'll be able to stop, and I don't want to end up sitting here talking to myself.

No. I know you wouldn't. Leaving was always my thing anyway, wasn't it? For what it's worth, I never meant for things to go the way they did. I never meant to hurt you. It's just that, well, what we had was good, you know? It felt right. And when things start to feel right it's like there's this little goblin inside of me who just wants to blow it all up just so it can be wrong again. I know that makes it sound like I'm not taking responsibility, like I'm some kind of victim. But I am. Taking responsibility, I mean. I hurt you and I never meant to hurt you. And I'm sorry.

So, yeah. The mannequins. That was her thing, right from the beginning. That very first day, before she ever said a word to me, she went right up to the one I had standing in the window. She had my sign in one hand and with the other she started adjusting. A little tug here, some smoothing out there. The skirt was askew. She fixed that. She put the sign in her teeth and did up the top button of its blouse, hiked up the stockings so the tops wouldn't show below the hem of the skirt, like she was protecting its modesty or something. Thing is, when she was done, the whole thing looked better. More than that, it looked *right*, like it had only been half-finished before, but once she was done, there was no other way that it could have been.

She made it her job without me ever having to say so, dressing the mannequin, making it to her liking. But more than that, she made sure that it was different every day. Me, I never bothered to change out its clothes more than once a week, and Lyden... Well, Lyden probably never noticed the thing at all. But to Poppy, well, it was everything.

Once I gave her the keys—which didn't take long. She was a good worker and I trusted her—but once I gave her the keys that mannequin was dressed and ready every single day before I even got there. Different clothes, different poses. Sometimes she'd even change the window dressing, make it into a little scene. I swear, half the time I didn't even recognize the things it was wearing. She must have brought them from home. I remember one time she had her dressed in a black tartan skirt like some kind of schoolgirl and there was a stack of books sitting in the window next to her. Old-timey shit with yellowed pages and worn bindings all tied up in a belt. I never did ask her where the books came from, but they were gone the next day.

She found two more of the things and put them up, too. When I asked her where she found them, she told me that they'd been in boxes way back in the storeroom. And maybe they were. I can't say for sure. But I'll tell you that I'd never seen them until that day, and I've managed that store long enough that I thought I knew every last thing in every corner. She set them up at the front of the store, not in the window, but one right by the entrance and the other off to the side by the lockup case. She did her best to keep them out of the way, but you've been there. You know how crowded that place is. You practically had to squeeze past them to move around. But that ended up being okay, because it meant that when people came in, they had to slow down, and that made them look at the mannequins, and when they did, they stopped, you know? Stopped and really looked at them. And every time you could see it on their faces, this little smile, this approval, because those mannequins were perfect, too. Poppy made them perfect every single day. Every day until...

I should probably back up a little. You know how I said that Poppy was bringing in the foot traffic? Well, it wasn't always good foot traffic. Sometimes when you have a store like that, people can sense when it's going to be chaos. Some people sense it, and decide that they want to take advantage of it. And those skater punks I mentioned before? Well, we started seeing more and more of them, and not in a good way.

It started with little things at first. I'd notice some of the energy shots that we kept on the counter had gone missing after they left. Or sometimes I'd find one of those blind-box character things torn open with the figure gone. Nothing I could prove, at least not right away, but I knew they were doing it. And they knew that I knew it too, the little shits. I think that was half the fun of it for them.

Poppy never seemed to notice them, though. Oh, she did her job. Did it well, too. Maybe better than anyone who's ever worked for me. But for her, everything revolved around those mannequins. It was almost like they were people to her. She'd greet them in the morning and say goodbye to them at night. Not in so many words. She never talked to them or anything like that. Nothing that set off any warning bells. I would have done something if there was. I would have taken her aside or at the very least tried to find out if she was okay, you know? I would have. I swear.

But it was almost like... almost like she was communicating with them somehow. She'd look right into their eyes—not that they had eyes, or faces, even. It was all just white plastic—and it was as if they just held her there. And she'd stare at them for a few seconds and then sometimes she'd nod or maybe even crack a little smile. I almost asked her about it once. I didn't though. I didn't want to sound like an idiot. Hell, I probably sound like an idiot now. But there was this... I don't know... *affinity* there. You could see it every time she passed them. She'd reach out and give them a little touch on the arm as she went, the way you might touch a friend. Or maybe a lover.

I'm sorry. This was a mistake. I shouldn't have asked you to come here. It's great that you did, but... I should have just left you alone. I didn't have the right. I should have just—

Yeah. Okay.

I suppose you're right. You've come this far. I'm glad you came this far. I really am. You deserve to hear the rest.

Things started to go bad when she found the box. I don't even know where it came from. This was about a month ago, and after those two mannequins showed up out of nowhere, I inventoried that entire storeroom and I swear never saw the thing before. It was old and faded, and you could see this jagged line from water damage all along its sides. Poppy was there standing over the thing, her shoulders slumped, her hair hanging down in her face. I don't think she heard me come in. I don't think it would have mattered if she had. I was afraid to go to her because as quiet as she was, the way she was standing there, it felt like I had walked in on a funeral.

It was another mannequin. In the box. At least, it was part of one. Just a head and a torso with a few more parts jumbled in. A hand snapped off at the wrist. A leg without a foot. Its face was caved in on one side, with a long, jagged scar that curved down from the forehead, across where its eye would have been and down into its mouth. The plastic all along that scar was melted, and it looked like a wound, like someone had done it on purpose. Worse, the plastic had curled and puckered as it pulled away from the gash in its face and looked for all the world like pale flesh. It looked so real. It looked almost human.

"Nothing ever lasts, does it?" That's what she said when she was standing over the box. She said it so softly that I couldn't tell if she was saying it to me or just to herself. "Nothing ever lasts, does it? You try to hold on, hold on for as long as you can. But all it ever does is break."

She might have been crying. I couldn't see her face, but I could hear it in her voice. Or maybe that's just the way I'm remembering it. In that moment she seemed every bit as fragile as that mannequin in the box, and maybe just as damaged. I wanted there to be something that I could say that would comfort her. I wanted to tell her that it was just a piece of plastic, but I think I knew even then that it wasn't exactly true.

In that moment, I wished that I wasn't her boss, because being her boss meant that I had to keep my distance. But I didn't want to keep my distance. I wanted to be her friend.

No. That's not quite true, either. You know how I said that it wasn't like that between me and Poppy? Well, there was a part of me that wanted it to be exactly like that. Not that I ever told her, no. Not that I ever even realized it until it was already too late. But I'd watch her with the mannequins. I'd see the way she looked at them, like she was seeing past the surface, past all that dead, cold plastic and into something that was vibrant and alive. Something that was real. I wanted someone to look at me like that. I wanted her to brush against my arm when she walked by like it was some secret language that only the two of us understood. I wanted her to see me better than I could ever see myself.

But I didn't say a word. Maybe if I had, things might have been different. Maybe they wouldn't have ended up the way they did. But I didn't say anything. I just backed away and closed the door. I left her there, alone, in the storeroom. I left her there because I was too much of a coward to tell her. After maybe an hour, it was like it never happened. She was back to her old self, chatting with the customers, smiling. That night I went back into the storeroom to see if I could find the box, but it was gone.

We didn't talk much after that. Not that that we talked all that much before, but there was a distance between us now. She didn't avoid me. Not exactly, anyway. But she kept to her work and always seemed to have a reason to be in the opposite corner of the store from the one that I was in. It was as if

I'd walked in on her while she was naked or something. Not because she was embarrassed or anything. I don't think she was. But I had seen something that I hadn't been meant to see. I was an outsider. I had gotten close, but all it meant was that now I was even farther away.

It was fall by then. Usually, we see more traffic right before Halloween, kids wanting to wear black, go goth for the holiday. Or maybe it was just that it got so cold and stayed cold, and the rain just wouldn't let up for days. And I know that they say that the whole thing about all the crazies coming out on the full moon is just an old wives' tale, but I'd swear to you it's true. It was a full moon the night that it happened.

I should have known there was trouble coming. The rain had forced all the skater kids inside, and that meant we were seeing them at least once a day, sometimes more. They'd linger near the front of the store, stick to the places where they could get out the door nice and quick. There were five of them, sometimes six. They'd wear these hoodies with the deep pockets in the front, made it easy to slip something big underneath and hold it there while they just strolled away. We could never afford the electronic security tags like the big department stores, so they kept getting away with it. I talked to mall security, but mall security didn't do a damn thing. Said they were short-handed but really, I think they just couldn't be bothered.

We lost a good twenty shirts in just a couple weeks. Lost a bunch of other stuff, too. Stupid stuff. Bracelets, socks, magnets. Anything that wasn't nailed down. Once they even took one of the holders we use for our markdown signs. It's like they didn't even care about the stuff, they just wanted to take it.

Got bolder too, as time went on. They figured out that they could pretty much have the run of the place as long as one or two of them kept us distracted. There was this one, a slouchy little bastard with red hair and crooked teeth, seemed to have an instinct for catching me off guard. He'd steal stuff right off the counter, look me dead-ass in the eyes while he was doing it, too. No fear. No shame.

They kept getting even bolder, too. We'd kick them out as soon as they walked in the door. They'd holler about their rights, how it was a free country, that they'd call the cops, their parents, anyone who'd listen. They'd leave but they'd be back the next day, maybe even in a few hours. It was a game now, and they weren't about to give it up just because I said so. Poppy kept her eye on them too. She was only a little thing, but she wouldn't hesitate to make them leave, just kind of standing in front of them with her arms folded until they finally went away. She was always pleasant about it—a lot more pleasant than I was—and it worked. At least for a while.

But the night it happened, that full moon night, they were back again. They were in the back of the store, where we keep all the novelty stuff. You know, the bachelorette party stuff. Gag gifts and handcuffs and little lollypops shaped like penises. There were four of them, and I was watching them as much as I could. They'd found the lacy panties we keep hanging on peg hooks and they were holding them up against their crotches, laughing like a pack of hyenas. I probably should have said something to them right then, but Poppy was at the front of the store, stocking some belts that we'd gotten in that morning, and truth be told I didn't want to stray too far from the register in case there was one more of them lurking around somewhere, just waiting for an opportunity. Anyway, I figured they'd lose interest soon enough, and the margin on the panties was so high that I figured it was almost worth losing a few pairs just to not have to deal with them.

I shouldn't have been worried about the register, though. That wasn't what they were after. But I knew they were up to something because all of a sudden, they got real quiet. They threw the panties back on the shelf and started drifting up toward the front of the store, toward the glass cases with all the headshop stuff inside, the high-ticket stuff. The redhead kid was at the center of it, taking the lead, and the rest of them fanned out around him, blocking my view of him, blocking the aisles even though there wasn't anyone else in the place apart from them and us. By the time I saw what they were up to, it was already too late to stop it.

It all happened pretty quick. I saw the redhead kid put his hand on the case and I was just about to yell at him to get the hell away from there when I heard this sharp bang, like a gun had gone off. That's when I saw what the kid had in his other hand. It was a little orange hammer with a metal tip, like the kind that you keep in your car to break the glass if you run off the road into a lake or whatever. That's all it took, just that one hit and the whole glass front of the case just shatters into pieces and crashes down all over the floor.

I jumped. The kids jumped. Poppy, up at the front of the store, jumped. The only one who didn't jump was that little red-haired bastard. All the noise got to the rest of them and they started to scatter, but not him. He knew exactly what he was after, and he reached up and took it, almost casual, like he was taking a cup down out of the cupboard. It was one of our high-end bongs. Blue glass. Hand blown. Maybe the most expensive thing in the whole store. Hell, if I'd have known what it would come to, I would have handed him the thing myself.

The other kids were out the door before he even started moving. He didn't even run. He just kind of *strode*, with the thing held out in front of him like some kind of trophy. Like he didn't have a care in the world. I think he was counting on all the noise and the chaos to keep us from doing anything about it until he was already free and gone. He must not have seen Poppy up at the front of the store. I don't know. Maybe he just didn't care.

She moved quick though, so quick that it seemed like she just appeared right in front of the doorway. The kid saw her there and he put his shoulder down, picked up speed. I guess he figured she'd just have to get out of his way. I wish to God that she had, but she wouldn't budge. She was small, but she still stared him down, all narrowed eyes and legs set like they'd grown roots right into the floor. I don't know what got into her. Maybe she'd just had enough. Maybe it was something about the sound of all that breaking glass. I don't know. But by the time the kid saw that she wasn't going to get out of his way, he was going too fast to stop. Not that he would have. He knew he was caught, but he wasn't going to stay caught. No, he was going out that door, one way or another.

Poppy saw it, too. I watched her eyes go wide. I was stuck behind the counter, too far away to do anything about it, even if I could have gotten my legs to move. He put his shoulder down, and he had the blue-glass bong tight against his chest like he was a football player or something. He made a move like he was going to duck around her, try and get under her arm and out the door. But she didn't move. Why didn't she just move? It was just some overpriced bullshit. Insurance would have covered it, that and the damage, too. All she had to do was get out of his way.

But she didn't get out of his way, and he didn't get around her either. He hit her arm, hard enough that it spun her around. He stumbled, and fell against the doorframe hard enough that it knocked the bong right out of his hands. Poppy went spinning. She tried to grab onto something, but she was too off balance and there was nothing there anyway. Nothing but the mannequin that Poppy had stood up by the door.

She backed right into it, and it rocked back on its stand. For a second it kind of paused there, and I was sure that it was going to rock right back and stay standing. It paused, but then it kept going. Poppy realized what was happening and kind of turned in midair, like she thought she could stop it. But she couldn't stop it. She didn't seem to care that she was falling, too. Once she saw that mannequin going over, it was like it was the only thing she could see. She reached out, but her fingers only brushed against it, and pushed it over even harder.

Its arm hit the shelf first, and I heard this loud crack, like the sound when you drop a plate on the floor. Up until then, I had thought that it was just made of hollow plastic like the one in the window. But I'd never touched it; only Poppy had. It was made of porcelain, or something like it. Something brittle enough that when its arm hit that shelf it snapped right off, halfway to the elbow. And when it did, the look on Poppy's face... It was like something inside her broke, too.

The mannequin's leg snapped off below the knee when it hit. The other one went right after. The stand with the legs attached kind of wobbled back upright, but the body just kept going. Poppy managed to get to it. She got her arms around it and she followed it down. She pulled it close and tried to turn herself so that she'd take the worst of the fall, like she was protecting a child. It didn't make any difference. When its head hit the floor, it sounded less like a plate and more like breaking glass, like a Christmas ornament that fell off the tree. It shattered, and as Poppy fell down next to it, she started to scream.

And the sound of that scream. My god, I can still hear it. She screamed so long and so loud that you'd think that the world was ending around her. And maybe it was. She pulled the pieces close and curled herself around them. The screams turned into crying. I've never heard anyone cry like that before, with so much anger and sadness and helplessness all balled up together. It was like it had been there inside her the whole time, just waiting for something to bring it all out.

I realized something then that, deep down, I think I had known all along. I just hadn't wanted to admit it, because even saying it now seems so ridiculous. But those mannequins weren't just hollow plastic and cracked porcelain. Not to Poppy, at least. No, they were real people, as real as you. As real as me. They had lives. They were loved. They were as close to

Poppy as any living person could be, maybe even closer, and now one of them was gone.

The dumb red-haired kid, he didn't know what to do. He just laid there in the doorway with his mouth hanging open like a fish in a rowboat until he finally decided he needed to get out of there. He didn't even bother to take the bong he'd tried to steal. The bitch of it was, the thing wasn't even broken. Not even scratched. I could put it back on the shelf, but I don't think I ever want to see the thing again.

But once I saw the kid run away, I realized that I had been staring, too. I went over to her, and I knelt down next to her and pulled her close. I pulled her close and I held onto her. I sat on the floor and I rocked her in my lap, and it took a while but eventually she stopped crying and I wiped some of the tears away from her eyes and she looked up at me and I...

No. I'm sorry. I don't know why I lied about that. I didn't do any of that. I wanted to, but I couldn't move. I just stood there behind the counter and watched. She was crying, and she was hurting and I couldn't bring myself to do anything about it. I just watched. I watched her cradle the pieces of the mannequin against her body, gathering them, almost like she thought that she could put them back together somehow. But she couldn't, and as her cries settled down, I could see the realization of it on her face. All her soft-hearted openness was gone, and in its place was something as hard and as brittle as the broken porcelain she was holding. Then, without a word, she stood up with all those pieces in her arms, and ran out the door.

I don't know how long it took me to go after her, but by the time I got past the mess and outside, she was long gone.

There were bits of porcelain on the ground, little shards of mannequin that told me which way she ran. I tried to follow them, but didn't get far. I thought about calling the police, but what was I going to tell them? About the theft, yeah. Only, it wasn't a theft anymore because the kid didn't take anything and they weren't going to waste any time on some small-time vandalism. About Poppy? Well, what was I going to say? That I was worried about her? That I was afraid for her? I was, but why would they care about that? Upset and alone is just par for the course. Everyone's like that all over. Who's going to give a damn about one more?

I didn't go to her right away. At least I can be honest with you about that much. A part of me thought that maybe I wouldn't go to her at all. But I couldn't stop looking at that mannequin stand with the broken legs on it. The more I looked at it, the more ashamed I felt. Maybe I could have done something to stop all of this before it happened, you know? Maybe if I had just been harder on those kids and thrown them out of the place, stood in the doorway so they couldn't come inside... I don't know. All I know is that the more I looked at those porcelain legs, the more shame I felt. They were broken, but still beautiful in their own way, like the ruins of some old Roman statue. Like all that was left of something that used to be wonderful.

I left the broken glass where it was, but I took those legs with me. It took a while before I could separate them from the metal stand, but got the wires out without breaking them more. I wrapped them in t-shirts so they wouldn't get any worse. I had Poppy's address from her application. It wasn't far. Walking distance, really, but I took my car and I drove it slow because every bump in the road made me afraid that the mannequin legs would shatter, that this time there wouldn't be any question that it really was my fault.

Poppy's apartment was on the second floor of one of those old factory buildings that they converted into lofts about twelve years ago. They'd left the old brick walls but cut more windows into the side of it, and you could see the faded letters above the doorway where the old sign used to be. The floors were old wood, and they creaked under my feet. I took my time so I wouldn't trip and spill my bundle of legs all over the hallway. I don't know what I thought I was doing. They were broken, and no use to anyone anymore. Still, they felt precious somehow, and I had made them my responsibility. I figured I had to see it through.

Her place was at the end of the hall. The light outside was broken and the door wasn't locked. I think I knew that it wouldn't be, because I didn't even knock before I tried the doorknob. The door creaked open and I called out her name. She didn't answer.

I pushed my way in. It was dark and there wasn't any furniture, but the place wasn't empty. I could... feel them in there, you know? Even before my eyes adjusted to the dark, it was like they were watching me, tracking my every move. When I could finally see them, I saw them everywhere, slender figures, all of them in these elegant poses, like they'd been frozen in the middle of a dance.

Poppy had dressed most of them, dressed them so flawlessly that any one of them would have been a star in that front window. Some of them stood there in nothing but their own skin. Those were the ones that stood out because they were perfect all on their own. The others were just cheap plastic, but these... these you could tell were much older. They weren't white, but a deep, bone yellow, and you could trace the cracks in their porcelain glaze like varicose veins. It was like they had never been meant to be used, only seen. A few had broken fingers. One was missing an arm. Another, a head. But they were all beautiful. Walking among them, I felt like I was walking into a room full of ghosts.

There was only a little light spilling out from under the bathroom door. I didn't want to go in, because I already knew what I was going to find there. I put down the bundled-up legs, right down at the feet of one of those old mannequins. Like an offering. It sounds stupid, I know, but it seemed right. It seemed like that's exactly where they belonged.

The floor was made of these cheap black and white tiles. Everything was wet and the cracks between them had gone all red. The bathtub was full and there was Poppy, just lying there in the middle of it. She had two long gashes down the lengths of her forearms. Whatever chance I'd had of helping her was lost before I'd ever gotten there. Maybe even before I'd let that mannequin get smashed to pieces in the store. I stood there in the doorway for a long time, just looking at her. One of her hands dangled over the edge of the tub and I listened to the slow drip falling from her fingers to the tile floor. The edges of her wounds had drawn inward, and they looked almost melted, the way the mannequin in the box had looked melted. Her eyes were still open, but her face was so...

peaceful, you know? So still, like all her cares had drained away with the blood. I touched her skin and it was cool. It was white as porcelain.

No, stop. You don't have to say that. I am to blame. I've already accepted that and I don't need you to... I don't know... *absolve* me of it. That's not why I asked you to come here. You didn't have to come here, but you did. That means the world to me. It tells me that maybe not everything I've broken is going to stay that way.

And no, I didn't call the police. Poppy didn't have anyone who cared about her. No one except me, I guess. And I really *do* care about her. I don't think I knew how much until I started to tell you about her. But I do. I care about her as much as she cared about the broken mannequin in that box, as much as she cared about the one that she watched get shattered into pieces.

That's why I couldn't call the police, you see. They'd just take her away, zipper her into a bag and leave her there until they could get away with burying her in some cardboard box in a shallow grave. And what would happen to the rest of them, then? They'd end up in the landfill, crushed to powder underneath tons of old banana peels and used condoms and who knows what else. I could stop all that, at least. It wasn't enough, but it was still something.

So, I brought all of them back to the store. It took me all night, but I managed to get them all set up, every single one of them, even the broken ones. Especially the broken ones. There's barely any room left to walk, but that's okay because I'm not letting anyone in, and if I see that red-haired kid any-

where near the place, I'm going to put my foot right up his ass.
They're safe with me now. They're safe, and they're beautiful.

And Poppy? She's the most beautiful of them all. I put her
right in the window, up front where everyone can look at her. I
used the stand that was left over from the one that was broken.
It took me a while to get the wires right, but at least with all the
blood gone I couldn't make too much of a mess of it. I dressed
her in the same black skirt she had worn on that first day. I put
her hand on her hip and her other arm out just so. I left her eyes
open, and I swear she's never looked more alive. You'll come
see her, won't you? I need you to see her. I need everyone to
see her.

Interlude

"IT'S PROBABLY JUST A rash," my wife said, though I could tell, even then, that she knew it wasn't true. I could hear it in her voice, the subtle rise at the end that almost made it a question. Her eyes had gone wide, just a little, but the boy never saw it. He was looking up at me with wide eyes of his own, eyes that wanted reassurance. Below them, the tip of his nose burned an angry red, like a pale shoulder left too long in the sun, like a lobster left to boil.

"Probably, yeah," I told him. "Just don't scratch at it or you'll make it worse, okay?"

The boy nodded, and his mother smoothed his hair back. It was a gentle touch, meant to calm them both, and it did, for a moment. But the troubled look returned as soon as his back was turned, and it did not go away.

Later that day, when he stepped off the school bus, I could see at a distance that the rash wasn't a rash at all. The whole of his nose had turned bright red, and the skin had stretched taut over the swelling all the way from the bridge to down around his nostrils.

"It's okay, dad. It doesn't hurt." As if to prove it, he took hold of his nose and wrenched it back and forth until his mother pulled his hand away.

"I can't believe your teacher didn't send you to the nurse," she said, and when she spoke there was a tremble in her voice. "I'm going to call her and ask her why she didn't send you to the nurse."

I placed a hand on her shoulder and she pressed her own down on top of it, squeezing hard. "If it's not better by tomorrow," I said, "we'll go see the doctor, okay?"

The boy frowned and nodded before he bounded up the stairs to his room. I watched him go. Later, when the rest of the house was asleep, I stood outside his door and listened to the soft sounds of his snoring.

At the doctor's the boy sat on the examination table, shirtless and shivering. He seemed little more than skin and bones, knobby joints held at awkward angles. The doctor took his temperature and prodded at his nose with latex fingers. He squeezed, and when he let go it gave off a high squeal, like a balloon leaking air, like the horn on a bicycle. He left the boy sitting alone on the table while he herded us into the hallway and spoke to us in hushed tones.

We took him out of school a week later. A group of kids had thrown him to the ground and tried to pull his nose from his face. It had grown round as a plum and as red as a fire engine and they said he must be faking it. But he wasn't faking. Already blue circles had darkened around his eyes and the skin around his mouth had gone red. The school offered apologies but ultimately did nothing. They knew it wasn't contagious, but still they were glad to see him gone.

He found my wife's old straw hat with the silk daisy in the band and took to wearing it wherever he went. Over the weeks he filled out some, but still not enough to fit in the threadbare checked coat that he pulled from a box in the garage. We'd try to dress him in the clothes that we had bought for him. A child's clothes. My son's clothes. Every time we would find him later in baggy pants held up with suspenders, in oversized shoes tied tight to too-small feet.

There was a wood across the street from where we lived then. It crouched at the edge of the blacktop, thick with brush and leafless saplings that stood like bristles between the narrow trees. On windy nights we could hear the branches clacking together like old bones, and the boy knew not to play there. And yet, he would turn his head toward that place at times when the breeze kicked up. On those nights, the sound through the trees became a low whistle, almost like music.

His skin turned pale and waxen, fading into a bleached white that felt slippery beneath my fingertips. One night I woke to find light leaking beneath the bathroom door. The boy sat sleepy in his pajamas on the edge of the tub while my wife scrubbed at his face with a washcloth. The cloth had gone white but his face would not come clean. I took her hand and held it still, and I sent him back to bed. We sat together on the tile floor, she and I, and I held her until she was finished crying.

I left my job to be with him then. Each day seemed to burn away like morning mist and no one could tell us how many we had left. I sat on the porch and watched him run across the yard in his floppy shoes, hitching up his trousers as he rolled his way through pratfalls. Sometimes he would stop at the edge of the yard to stare across the street at that thicket of trees. He did not speak any more. Every communication was in a broad and elaborate pantomime. There were times when he would look at me and I could see in his eyes that there was something he needed me to understand. It was all right, because I already knew.

He became a restless, nocturnal creature, shunning the day-light, angling lampshades in a darkened room to turn them into spotlights. The doctor had given my wife pills to help her sleep, so she did not hear him when he would sneak into the garage at night. I'd watch him, unseen, from behind the gap in the open door while he balanced one-legged on a bucket, juggling garden tools with the ease of a master. I'd watch him and wonder how much of my boy was left there, beneath the carrot-orange hair, behind the oversized smile. I'd watch him grow still and cock his head toward the street and the woods beyond. In those moments, I could hear the distant sounds of a calliope on the air.

My wife barely spoke of him anymore, barely acknowledged his presence when he came tripping and honking into the room. Though I wanted to, I could not blame her. She had known what his changes would mean long before I did, but her mourning still loomed like a living thing. When she sat on the bed, a book of old photos in her lap, I could not join her. Not while our son was still where I could touch him. Not while I could still look into his eyes, eyes that had stayed the same when there was so much of him I no longer recognized.

On that night, that last night, I woke from a fitful sleep to find that he was no longer in the house. Panicked, I ran to the yard, the screen door banging behind me. I found him at the edge of the lawn, in the coat that was no longer mine, in the hat he had made his own. He was staring across the street, at the woods. There, between the trees, I saw them. They peeked out from behind the branches. Jangling harlequins in drooping hats. Grinning augustes with wide, red smiles. Sad Pierrots in ruffled collars. Their pale faces caught the light, gathering it up and reflecting it like little moons. All of them were watching. All of them were waiting.

My boy turned to me then, no longer my boy but something else, something that I could no longer hold. There was a question in his eyes, eyes that still held in them everything of the boy I had once known. I nodded my answer, and a smile worked its way across his face, a smile familiar and alien all at once. Then he turned to the forest, running to join his brethren there as they jangled their bells to welcome him.

I felt my wife come up behind me. She slid beneath my arm and we watched him go until we could no longer see him through the trees. Tears spilled from her eyes in the silence, but I could see that she was smiling. I realized then that I was smiling, too. We held each other in the dark, and listened to the wind blowing through the branches. On it, we could hear the fleeting sounds of laughter.

The Stumblybum Imperative

"Mommy, can we get more kays?"

Carol's eyes fluttered open. She hadn't been asleep, not all the way, but near enough that it took her a moment to understand why Sophie, and the rest of the world, had turned sideways.

"What's that, sweetie?"

"Can we get more kays?" The little girl paused for a moment, searching her brain, then added, "please?"

Carol pushed herself up from the table—empty coffee cup with a ring in the bottom, a stack of bills waiting to be paid—and looked down at the expectant little face framed in a tangle of unruly hair. She smiled, and wished that it was easier to smile. "I'm sorry, honey. I don't know what that means."

Sophie's eyes narrowed, confused at what she had no doubt thought was a carefully worded request. Carol could almost see the wheels turning behind her eyes as she considered her options. It was a serious look, an adult look, almost too adult for her five-year old face.

"Mister Mudgett said the Toyman's coming so we need more kays in the TV."

Mister Mudgett. Carol had heard the name before. She sighed and smiled her most patient smile. "Sweetie, I'm sure Mister Mudgett says a lot of things, but he's only make-believe."

"I know, but..." Sophie frowned, with more than a hint of I'm-not-stupid indignation. "But he said for real that we should get more kays for when the Toyman comes to Humblyburg and I wanna see all the colors."

Her eyes softened then, pleading. It was blatant manipulation, but they both knew that Carol was powerless against it. "Please, Mommy?"

She reached out and touched Sophie's cheek, her face so grown up and full of resolve. She'd been looking into that face since the day she first held her, and it was still a surprise when she found something new in it. "I'll take a look, okay?"

"Promise?"

"I promise I'll take a look," Carol said. Sophie smiled and skipped away satisfied, humming a tune that seemed familiar, though Carol couldn't quite place it. She watched her daughter go, curls bouncing as she turned and disappeared into the living room. Apart from the muffled voices from the television, the place was quiet, so quiet that it seemed almost empty. She stared at the ring in the bottom of the coffee cup and thought to make herself another. But the pot was all the way over on the counter by the sink and might as well have been on the other side of the moon. She laid her head down on the table and closed her eyes, but did not sleep.

"No, it's fine. I just... well, I didn't realize."

"It's not a big deal. I can come back later if it's not a good time."

The kid stood on the concrete stoop on the other side of the screen door, sun-blond hair and faded, grass-stained jeans. He looked past her as he talked, disinterested in that way that teenagers seemed to adopt almost by instinct. She turned around to see what he was looking at. Ketchup bottle on the table with the cap off. Butter knife sticking out of the mayonnaise jar. Drips on the table that ran together into smeary pink fingerprints.

"No, it's fine." She ran a hand over her face, suddenly aware of the fraying edges of her t-shirt, of the stains on her gray yoga pants. "It's just... how much did you say it was again?"

"Seventy. Thirty for the lawn and five for trimming the weeds. I tried ringing the bell last week but no one answered."

Last week might not have happened at all for as much as Carol remembered of it. If he had rung the bell then, would she have even heard it? She had barely heard it this time, and she hadn't heard the mower at all.

"Like I said, I can come back." He was looking at her face now, young eyes full of sympathy. Or was it pity? How old was this kid? Sixteen, maybe seventeen? After everything that Shaun had put her through, she was not about to let herself be pitied.

She straightened, and tried on a look that she thought might be a smile. "It's fine," she said, a little more quickly than she meant to. "I just... Just give me, like, two minutes."

She left him on the doorstep and hurried out of the kitchen into the living room. She buried her face in her hands. She wanted to scream, but she couldn't summon the energy. She hadn't screamed, hadn't even cried, since the day that Shaun had left them and she wouldn't let the kid who mowed the lawn be the thing that got her going now. Still, it was just like Shaun to not have told her, to leave her standing on the doorstep feeling stupid, not knowing how much they paid to have their lawn cut or even what day it was.

She pressed her palms against her eyes, hard enough to see red. When she brought them away, Sophie was there, on her knees in front of the TV. On the little screen, brightly colored figures danced in a circle, led by a mass of purple yarn in a top hat. Their steps were out of time with the music, the camera tilted at an odd angle like some old art film.

Sophie craned her neck back to look at her. "Are you ok, Mommy?"

Carol smiled, and didn't have to force it this time. She reached down and touched her daughter's chin. "I'm fine sweetie. You doing ok?"

Sophie nodded and turned back to the screen. The one in the top hat lurched and tugged, urging them to move faster. The circle broke and collapsed in on itself in a tangle of plush and felt-covered limbs. "I want to see stuff like Mister Mudgett, but I can't because we don't have enough kays for the TV."

"More kays. Sure." Already she was rummaging through the little vase where they kept their emergency cash. There was plenty, for now at least, though she didn't know when she'd be able to put more in. She hadn't heard from Shaun since the day he'd left, but he hadn't touched the bank account, and that was something at least.

"I only have twenties for now," she said, raising her voice as she hurried back into the kitchen, "so you can keep— Damnit."

One of the bills fell from her hand and she bent low at the waist to pick it up. When she straightened, she caught the kid's eyes drifting toward her rear end and then snapping back. As she opened the screen door, she thought she could see a flush of heat rising in his cheeks. He might be seventeen, maybe even eighteen.

"I only have twenties, so you can keep the change. But..." She cast a glance over her shoulder at Sophie, edging closer to the TV in the other room. "But I don't think I can keep paying you to do the lawn. You see, my husband... Well, I don't know what he arranged with you, but he's not... I mean, I'm not..."

"It's ok," he said. His face was impassive but his gaze wasn't wandering anymore. "I mean, it's not a big deal or anything."

"Thanks," she said, wishing that she hadn't mentioned Shaun, or that he had even come to mind at all. She turned once more to see Sophie, hair bouncing as she shifted and swayed to the music from the TV. When she turned back, the kid was gone from the stoop and walking down the sidewalk, dragging his mower behind him.

———◇———

Carol measured the passing of days by the unwashed dishes in the sink, by the unpaid bills that gathered in a stack by the door. Today, she told herself each day, would be the day to tend to the laundry that flowed out of its basket in Sophie's room, to vacuum the stray crumbs that had gathered on the carpet. But when the day's light faded, she always found herself in her place on the couch, staring sideways at the long shadows cast through the window.

When she moved at all, it was always for Sophie. Her needs were few and easy to tend to, and they were always enough to bring Carol to her feet, even if it meant being pulled upright by little hands. She would draw her baths and make her grilled cheese sandwiches, and Sophie would eat them, never complaining, even when the edges were burnt. At night Sophie would crawl next to her on the couch and pile the blankets around them. With Sophie sitting close, her tablet in her lap, Carol could almost forget the day's failures. She could almost believe that everything was back to normal.

"Whatcha watchin' there, baby?"

Sophie didn't look up from her screen, but she nudged herself deeper into the crook of Carol's hip. "The Stumblybums."

The screen was awash with bright colors as the characters huddled in their costumes in front of a background of orange and pink stripes. Oversized heads made of felt and foam pressed together, barely fitting inside the frame. At their center, a character in a yellow costume was on its knees, hands pressed in anguish to the sides of its bald and bumpy head, though its face was still smiling.

"He looks unhappy." Carol studied her daughter's face, lit from below in the glow of the tablet, watching her reactions.

"That's Gib," Sophie said, her eyes barely blinking. "He's always in trouble."

"Oh?" Carol bundled Sophie in closer, feeling protective but not knowing why. "What did he do?"

Sophie sat quiet for a time, listening to the tinny voices from the tablet's speaker. Gib was sobbing a loud "Boo-hoo-hoo," his voice high, like a woman's. Carol thought that it probably *was* a woman under all that cloth, behind the wide eyes that rolled with every movement of its head. Oversized hands patted Gib's shoulders and tried in vain to pull him to his feet.

"He told another fib and now he's afraid that the Numblycrumbs are going to get him."

"I thought *he* was a Numblycrumb."

Sophie rolled her eyes. "No, he's a Stumblybum," Sophie said, leaning into the word, like it should have been obvious.

"Then what's a Numblycrumb?"

Sophie reached out a tiny finger and touched the corner of the screen. She left an oily print behind, but beneath it Carol saw a spot beyond the characters where the stripes didn't quite line up, a vague human outline in a costume made to match the background. It crept forward, arms raised, hopping from foot to foot.

"*That's* a Numblycrumb. They like wrongthoughts," Sophie said, her voice small and distant. "If you think too many wrongthoughts, the Numblycrumbs come and they find you."

The striped thing was on them now, looming tall behind the other characters. None of them turned to see it, but they seemed to know it was there because they parted at its approach, shrinking back to leave Gib on his knees, alone and wailing.

"And what happens if it finds you?"

As if in answer, the thing pressed its hands down on Gib's shoulders. Its head began to shake, trembling violently, as if it were having a seizure. Its hands crept to Gib's neck and he began to shake too, his giant head rocking from side to side, his eyes rolling.

Carol held her breath as the Numblycrumb twitched, its movements quick and jerky, like a sped-up film, though everything around it moved at normal speed. Its hands slid along Gib's neck, beneath the heavy felt of his costume, and then Gib was twitching too.

The striped hands worked quickly, almost too quick to see. They darted beneath the great foam head and back again, knocking it off kilter, spinning it sideways. The music rose, a calliope punctuated by slide whistles and the twang of springs, desperate to turn the scene into a comedy. Sophie laughed, high and clear, like the ringing of a bell, and threw her head back so hard that the tablet almost fell to the floor. Carol tried to laugh, too. She wanted to trust the music, but nothing about what she was seeing seemed funny.

At last the Numblycrumb let go of Gib and backed away, shifting from leg to leg, hopping as it went. Gib no longer held his hands to his ears, and though his eyes still goggled and rolled with every movement of his head, Carol imagined that she could see relief in them.

Sophie squealed in delight. "He ate all the wrongthoughts! Did you see, Mommy, did you see?"

"Yes, honey. I saw." Now that her daughter has said it, the Numblycrumb *had* seemed to be eating, shoveling handfuls of something from beneath Gib's head into a mouth that was not there. Carol frowned, and felt at once like a voyeur, as if she were witnessing something she had never been meant to see. Gib's friends were back now, helping him to his feet. The Numblycrumb retreated, walking backward, melting into the backdrop as if it had never been there.

"Mister Mudgett says we need to see all the colors to find the Numblycrumbs, and that's why we need more kays."

"Which one's Mister Mudgett?"

Again, Sophie pressed a finger to the screen. This time it landed on a dark figure that lurked in the background at the edge of the frame. It was covered in purple yarn that coiled like dreadlocks and wore a crumpled stovepipe hat atop what might have been its head. Carol squinted because she had not seen him there until now, and now that she did, she didn't know how she could have missed him.

"Can we get more kays, Mommy? Please?"

"Sure, sweetie." Carol ran her fingers absently through Sophie's thick curls. "But right now, it's past your bedtime."

"Aww." Sophie protested but set the tablet aside anyway. Carol pulled her close, and Sophie squealed as she tickled her stomach.

"I love you, pumpkin," Carol said, and leaned in close until their noses mushed together.

"I love you too, Mommy." Sophie was smiling, but for an instant Carol saw a darkness cross her eyes, as if this moment, the joyful normalcy of it, had only served to illuminate how abnormal the past few weeks had been.

"I want Daddy back."

"I do too, pumpkin." It was a lie, but she made herself smile as she said it. She could see him in Sophie's face sometimes, in the way her mouth turned down when she was deep in thought. He was there in the way her jaw clenched when she was angry, and Carol worried that one day she might grow to hold that against her.

"But now," Carol said, tapping her daughter on the nose, "you have to go and brush your teeth."

"Nope." Curls of hair bounced around Sophie's face as she giggled.

"Yes, and make sure you do a good job this time. Up, down and all around, got it?"

"*Fine.*" She drew the word out as she trudged toward the hallway, mock stomping giving way to a run. With one last bounce of her hair she turned the corner, and Carol was alone in the quiet room. Only, she didn't feel alone, for the tablet lay in her lap on pause with the screen still glowing, the dark figure of Mister Mudgett and his top hat frozen in the corner. If she didn't know better, she might have sworn he was staring at her.

"I thought we said you weren't going to do the lawn anymore."

She hadn't planned on coming outside in the sweatpants and t-shirt she'd been living in for the past three days. Now that she had, she knew it was a mistake. She had to squint against the sun that felt too hot on her shoulders. The gravel driveway crunched and stabbed at her bare feet.

The kid saw her coming. He killed the mower's engine and plucked out his earphones to let them dangle against his chest.

Carol straightened and tried to look stern. "I'm sorry. I thought we'd said last time that you didn't need to do the lawn anymore."

The kid shrugged and thrust his hands into his pockets. "It's not a problem, really. I was out at the Stantons' anyway, and your yard isn't all that big, so I thought..."

He didn't say the rest. He didn't have to, because she had seen him take in the state of her clothes, her unwashed hair. He thought that they needed charity. The worst part was, he might be right.

She folded her arms, blew the stray hairs from her face and tried to smile. "I mean, I don't want to sound ungrateful. I am. Grateful, that is. It's just that... well, I wouldn't feel right taking advantage of you like that."

He opened his mouth to speak but Carol raised a hand to stop him. "So, I'll pay you for this week. How much did you say it was?"

"You don't have to—"

She stopped him with a look. It was a look she used on Sophie sometimes, when she wasn't listening and needed to know who was in charge.

"Thirty," he said.

Carol smiled, and felt it this time. "Thirty, then. I can pay you thirty for this week, but after that... It's just that I have to keep an eye on things. Finances and such. You understand, right?"

The kid nodded.

"Okay. We can settle up when you're done. I'll be in the kitchen."

It took him longer than she'd thought it would. She'd put her head down to rest and by the time he rapped on the screen door she was asleep at the kitchen table, a twenty-dollar bill and two fives crumpled tight in her fist.

"I can help, you know."

She rubbed at her eyes and pulled a stray strand of hair from her mouth. "Help with what?"

"My aunt had some trouble too, after my uncle died. Stayed in bed for days, wouldn't answer the door."

From the other room came the too-loud sound of the television, the Stumblybums singing their theme song, the song she knew by heart now. Her senses were on alert, with this strange man in her kitchen—for he was old enough to think of as a man, and taller than she was. He was standing in her kitchen and she hadn't invited him to come in.

"It's nothing to be ashamed of, really," he said, a little too quickly. Lots of people have it, and I hate to see..."

He glanced toward the short hallway that lead to the living room, to where Sophie sat, too close to the TV. Mister Mudgett, all top hat and yarn dreadlocks, filled the screen. He was muttering something Carol couldn't understand, but Sophie was listening to him closely, and she was smiling.

"I mean... Well, here." He fished deep in the front pocket of his jeans and pulled out a little plastic bag. Inside it was a cluster of little pills.

"I don't need them anymore. I had a bunch left over because our insurance was pretty decent and my mom kept refilling the prescription. When I told her I wasn't taking them anymore, she thought I tossed them, but..."

They were little capsules, blue and white, and the bag that held them caught the light as the kid turned it over in his hand. Carol cast an anxious glance down the hallway, but Sophie was still entranced by Mister Mudgett, her curls dancing as she bounced up and down on her knees.

"They work," the kid said. "I can vouch for that myself. And they work, like, right now. You won't have to wait."

She stared up at the kid, saw that he had stepped closer.

"How much?"

The kid shrugged, hands in his pockets. "At school I get eight per, but I can let you have them for six." So, it wasn't charity after all. She frowned and looked back at her daughter, at her face glowing with the light from the TV screen. She was a bad mother, she thought, and not for the first time.

"I'll throw in the yardwork for free."

The kid was smiling now. It was a smile that went all the way up to his eyes. The pills glittered in their bag and saying no wouldn't make her any better.

She slid the crumpled bills across the table.

———————◄O►———————

The world seemed to open up to her, and it was like the sun had come out from behind the clouds after months of nothing but rain. The dishes in the sink were gone. They sat, washed and waiting in their cupboards. Gone too was the overflowing basket of laundry, the crumbs on the carpet, the blobs of toothpaste in the bathroom sink.

She'd sat at the kitchen table for more than an hour on that first day, staring down at the five pills lined up like little soldiers in front of her. The sounds of the Stumblybums drifted in from the other room, her daughter's high laughter rising above the music of calliope and theremin. It was only when the songs died away and the TV snapped off that she swallowed two dry without thinking. She swept the others into the bag and hid them in a box of tea bags up on one of the high shelves.

She had nearly forgotten she'd taken them when they bloomed inside her like a dried flower in water, spreading a warming glow out to her darkest corners. With it came a wild and urgent energy, a need to do everything all at once. It pulled her everywhere and nowhere at the same time. Later, when her racing heart had learned to slow, she rode the feeling like a wave, letting it carry her from room to room, lifting all the burdens that had seemed so insurmountable just hours before.

Sophie watched her as she worked, wary of this strange, new creature that had emerged in her mother's place. She kept her distance, but Carol still caught the amusement that began to creep into the corners of her daughter's mouth when she thought her mother couldn't see. She forgot her hesitation completely when Carol produced a pot of macaroni and cheese for lunch, a feat as close to real cooking as she'd attempted in weeks. They sat together on the couch with their bowls in their laps while Gib and Narly and Listabell—all names that surprised Carol with how easily they came to mind—danced and careened across the screen.

And while they sat, Carol looked at her daughter, *really* looked at her for the first time in as long as she could remember. There were smears of orange at the corners of her mouth and stains on the front of her oversized t-shirt, and yet, there was a quality in her eyes, a faraway thoughtfulness that seemed to add years to her tiny features. She wondered just how much her little girl had grown up in these weeks, with her father gone and her mother absent in everything but body. She wondered what Sophie had lost, and if she'd ever be able to get it back again.

She ran a finger through her daughter's curls, but Sophie didn't notice. Carol could feel her little body growing tense, and it made her stiffen too. Gib had been dancing on the screen just a moment before, a giant smile on his too-wide face. Only now the smile didn't match his movements. His arms flailed, gloved hands clawing at his throat as if he were gasping for air. Listabell went to him, the great pink bell of her costume bending back as she fought to steady him. Narly drifted off toward the edge of the frame. There was something in the hesitance of his steps that told Carol that they were seeing something that not even the actors under the costumes had expected, something that wasn't part of the script.

Sophie leaned toward the TV, holding her breath. Carol held her breath too as she watched Gib fall to his knees and start to shake. Listabell stumbled back. Carol was certain now that this was real, that something awful was about to happen to whoever was inside Gib's costume. His hands went again to his throat, pulling at the fabric. Carol thought at once of the Numblycrumb, of its jerking movements, of its hands creeping toward Gib's neck, but there was nothing there.

Gib gave a last little jump, as if something had punched him hard and knocked him off balance, before he collapsed to the floor. He didn't just fall down. Instead, the suit seemed to deflate, as if the person inside had shrunken away to nothing and left only empty felt and foam behind.

The camera tilted sideways, just for an instant, but it was enough to show the darkened edges of the stage where the trippy striped backdrop didn't reach. When it panned back it found Listabell. The camera zoomed in on her face, on the warm and innocent smile that had been drawn there beneath ever-twinkling eyes. Even under the plush and the glitter, Carol could see that she was trembling. The music had stopped. A hush had suffused its way through the set, a terrible stillness, a collective holding of breath.

The music came back, halting at first, a smattering of drum-beats, a too-fast tinkle of notes on a keyboard. The camera zoomed out. Gib was still on the ground, but he was moving now, rocking back and forth like a turtle on its back. Had she just imagined the way the costume had fallen, the way it had crumpled, empty, to the floor?

Sophie giggled, bouncing on her knees at the edge of the couch. "Gib fell down, Mommy!"

"Yes, honey," Carol whispered, unable to take her eyes from the screen. Listabell was jumping up and down and pumping her fists into the air. It was meant to show excitement, but the movements seemed desperate, and Carol read something in them that looked like like fear. "Gib fell down."

Narly rushed forward and made a show of pulling Gib to his feet, of smoothing the felt of his costume. He turned his single, unblinking eye to the camera and spread his arms as if he had just done a magic trick, as if everything they'd just seen had been expected. The camera reset itself to its accustomed distance, framing the characters against the orange-striped background, wrapping them in their familiar setting.

Only, there was something in the way that Gib moved that was not familiar at all. He took halting steps, like a child just learning to walk, and when he turned around, his arms flopped at his sides as if the bones had gone missing. He moved toward the camera and tilted his head, that manic smile still glowing, his felt eyes unblinking. When at last he spoke, it was a garble of sounds, deep and guttural, like something wet being eaten by a garbage disposal.

Sophie giggled and looked up at her mother with dancing eyes. "He sounds just like Mister Mudgett now!"

———◦———

Carol swung her legs out of bed and looked down at her feet in their mismatched socks. She couldn't sleep, not with Gib's frozen smile, more desperate each time it came to her, swirling through the eddies of her mind. Sophie seemed unburdened by such thoughts, and fell asleep with a smile on her face the moment her head hit the pillow. Carol's brain refused to quiet, and threw off all attempts at sleep like a wild and bucking horse.

She thought back to the pills but couldn't remember if she had taken three or only two. She wanted to pull one more from the little bag in its hidden place high on the kitchen shelf, but to do so would be as good as admitting that there would be no sleep tonight. Her stomach churned and cramped, and she wondered if she should eat something. Instead, she reached for her phone and told herself that it was only to check her emails. Shaun hadn't written. She hadn't expected him to. Sleep and food forgotten, she thumbed open her browser, scrolling through screen after screen, falling into the deep well of the Internet.

The Internet, it turned out, knew all about The Stumbly-bums.

Through blog post after blog post, Reddit threads and wiki entries, she was able to piece together the history of the show. It had begun life as what one review had called "a forced and utterly forgettable kids show, generic in its outlook and lacking in educational and entertainment value." After watching a few clips of those early episodes, she could see the reviewer's point. Each one was the same: five characters in cheap-looking plush suits bungling their way through learning to share, singing songs about self-esteem and keeping their hands to themselves. Watching over them was a rotund little man in a baggy red suit and a black top hat called Ringmaster Reggie. Ringmaster Reggie represented the show's moral center, an adult presence that shepherded the plush-costumed characters from one learning opportunity to the next. The whole thing played out live, four times a week from twelve-thirty to two.

Until the day that Ringmaster Reggie disappeared.

It happened without any announcement or narrative fore-shadowing. He had simply been there one episode and was gone the next. If the show had been at all popular, the trade papers might have made a note of it, but after only 23 episodes The Stumblybums was already well into its downswing. The critics who watched in retrospect all agreed that the down-swing would have continued into television obscurity had it not been for Ringmaster Reggie's replacement, Mister Mud-gett.

Mister Mudgett arrived in the very next episode after Reg-gie's last, wearing the very same black stovepipe hat atop dark purple tangles of yarn. The Stumblybums' stories didn't change, but where Ringmaster Reggie had been a gentle hand, guiding the characters with praise and affection, Mister Mud-gett was a fist. If Narly forgot to brush his tooth or Listabell played too rough and broke Gib's toy, Mudgett responded in a fury, flailing his fists and sometimes kicking over parts of the set as he ranted, always in the same crushed-gravel non-sense-speak. It was pure slapstick, and it was the shot in the arm that the show needed. In the weeks that followed, ratings began to rise.

It didn't take long for this new incarnation of The Stumbly-bums to become a cult hit. Clips of the show were posted online and went viral within hours. Adults and teenagers came to it in droves, and it became the show of choice to watch while getting high. Kids started watching again too, and while the behavioral experts bemoaned the show's reliance on violence and cheap laughs over values and education, The Stumbly-bums was more popular than ever.

Over time, with Mudgett in charge, the show began to change. The characters trudged through their usual morality plays at first, tiptoeing around Mister Mudgett as if afraid to catch his ire. Over time, the stories became more and more inaccessible, abandoning all pretense of education in favor of spiraling plotlines that were abandoned abruptly in one episode only to be picked up again weeks later. Internet obsessives pored over every show, pulling the threads together, confident in some hidden meaning that would reveal itself with enough time and attention. Wikis and analysis videos blossomed. The ratings continued to soar.

Rumors began to swirl around the show's creators, a group of improv actors from Dayton, Ohio who left behind computer programming jobs for the thrill of basic cable. Whispers of sexual deviance and Satanic symbolism spread through social media, whispers that took hold in mainstream media outlets and drew the ire of religious organizations. The rumors intensified when Brad Foreman, the show's head writer and the performer behind Tink-a-Bink, a tall and often haughty flower that was the fifth member of the main Stumblybums cast, disappeared. Like Ringmaster Reggie, Tink-a-Bink left the show without warning, and like Ringmaster Reggie, the performer had disappeared in real life, without a trace.

The show's plotlines continued to spin wild like bumper cars, careening through pointless treasure hunts, rearranging of furniture, and measuring imaginary lines on the studio floor. But through it all was a single storyline, a constant thread upon which hung every action the Stumblybums took: the Toyman was coming, and they had to be ready for his arrival.

The Toyman had become the cause of much speculation in the online communities that had popped up around the show. His identity was as much a mystery as what would happen when he finally arrived. Some factions believed that he was just another Numblycrumb from Harshlytown. Others believed that he was coming to save Humblyburg and put an end to the Numblycrumbs once and for all. Still others argued that Mudgett was merely the Toyman in disguise. Theories abounded, and Carol followed them down and down until the dawn light began to filter in through the window blinds. She checked the clock. It was nearly six in the morning. Sophie would be up soon, and Carol still had not slept.

She thought again of the little bag on the kitchen shelf, of the pills still left inside. What she needed, she knew, was sleep. Just a few hours. She could go to bed right now and be up in time to make Sophie lunch. Her daughter was old enough to fend for herself for a few hours. It would only be a few hours.

But what if it wasn't? a little voice asked. What if she slept all day and left Sophie all alone? It was Shaun's voice. It was the voice of Mister Mudgett, all gravel and wet leaves. It could happen, she knew. It had happened before.

She could take just one, she thought as she pulled the bag down and turned it over and over again between her fingers. The two she'd taken that morning had worn off by now, she was sure of it. If she took one now, it would leave two more that she could keep for an emergency, for some low, cloudy day when the weight of it all threatened to crush her all the way down to nothing. And it wasn't as if she was some junkie. Kids took these things all the time, every day. She just needed one. One to get through to the end of the day, that's all.

She put two in her mouth and swallowed them dry.

———•◦•———

"Mommy, where'd my tablet go?"

Carol didn't look up over the top of her phone. "What's that, sweetie?"

Sophie's face scrunched. "My tablet's gone, Mommy."

"Well, where did you see it last?"

She frowned, wheels turning. "On the couch, I think. But it's not there, Mommy. I looked."

"I'm sure it's wherever you left it last. Have you checked in your room?" Carol felt bad about the lie, but not bad enough to let it change her mind.

Sophie threw her head back and groaned. "I already looked there," she said, but stomped off down the hall anyway. Carol watched her go, still convinced, though a little less convinced now, that she had made the right choice. Sophie had been spending almost every waking hour with The Stumblybums, pulling up old episodes on the little screen, watching them over and over again until there were little red circles under her eyes. Carol didn't kid herself that she could win any parenting awards, but she was still enough of a mother to know that it had to stop. And it wasn't as if she had cut her daughter off entirely. Sophie could still watch the new episodes when they came on the television. With any luck, without the constant exposure, she'd find something completely different to obsess about in a few days.

It was a guilty thought, and the hypocrisy of it tugged at Carol's insides. Even now, she was scrolling through an article about The Stumblybums on her phone, an analysis of the costumes and set design of the first thirty-one episodes of the show, highlighting what the anonymous author called "clear and repeated symbolism drawn from the Lesser Key of Solomon." It came with much supporting evidence—zoomed-in images adorned with red circles and hand-drawn arrows—but there was no way for her to judge how convincing it was on such a tiny screen.

This had been her routine for the past six days and through the long weekend without any new episodes. The well of information on The Stumblybums was bottomless and the more she dug the deeper it drew her in. The disappearance of Brad Foreman and Ringmaster Reggie had seemed like a solvable problem at first, and one with a simple explanation that would set her mind at ease about all the rest. Instead she found a kaleidoscope of conspiracy theories. Most of them were mundane, webs of jealousy and foul play, rumors of infidelity and same-sex romance. But these were not the stories that interested her the most. The stories she gravitated to were the ones whose authors were only known by aliases, the ones that found homes on fringe sites and cited episode numbers and timestamps as proof. And all of them centered around the arrival of the Toyman.

Carol bookmarked webpages and scribbled notes on the backs of old receipts and any other scraps she could find. She listened to podcasts while she cleaned, scrubbing the bathroom tiles far longer than they needed while a long-form attempt to translate Mister Mudgett's croaking nonsense-speak played through her headphones. She had watched through the show's entire run, all 68 episodes, most of them twice, freeze-framing them according to the lists that she'd made, squinting at tiny details, zooming in until it all became lost in a blur of pixels.

Her searching and combing always, unfailingly, brought her back to the day that Gib changed. She hadn't been imagining things. Others online had noticed the boneless way his arms hung at his sides, the subtle shift in the set of his shoulders that made him look like he had no shoulders at all. After The Turn, which is what they'd taken to calling it after the initial shock had died down, Gib didn't move the same. His head pitched back at odd times and his feet shuffled as he walked. Once he started speaking Mudgett's odd language, his behavior became erratic and unpredictable. He bumped into scenery and wandered offstage at odd times, leaving Narly and Listabell to ad-lib around his actions. Once, while Listabell was giving a speech about eating vegetables, Gib stepped into the frame and stared close into the camera for a full twenty-three seconds. The conclusion was clear and it gained a consensus: whoever—whatever—was in that costume, it just wasn't Gib anymore.

A bang and a growl of frustration drifted out from Sophie's room. Carol would have to tell her about the tablet sooner or later, but now was not the time, not while Sophie was having a fit and definitely not when the bag with the little blue and white pills was empty.

The kid had left her his number. She hadn't thought then that she would need it, but she did. He'd been back once already, and she'd bought fifteen more of them with money she'd lifted from the emergency fund. They didn't last, and when she texted him again this morning he'd said he could be there by noon. The clock on her phone read 11:45. If he was on time, and he had been so far, there would be plenty of time to catch the new episode when it came on at 12:30.

Another crash rang out from the bedroom, followed by a long silence. Carol stilled her tapping foot and held her breath. Sophie was crying, not a pain cry but a low, steady sob of frustration and mourning. Carol wanted to go to her, to scoop her daughter up and hold her close, but the bell might ring at any moment. She stared at the clock and told herself that she would give the tablet back as soon as— As soon as what? As soon as it was safe, was her first thought, but she didn't want to ponder too long about what exactly that meant.

The doorbell rang, and Carol jumped up from her chair, a wad of bills clenched tight in her fist. When the transaction was done and the baggie full of pills hidden safely away, she crept down the hall and stood in the doorway to her daughter's room. Sophie sat at the center of an avalanche, books and toys and stuffed animals scattered all around. Her hair hung over her face and tears were drying in little tracks down her cheeks.

"The Stumblybums are going to be on in a minute," Carol said, and tried to smile as she held out her hand. "Come on. We can watch it together."

— ◇ —

They watched all the new episodes together now, Sophie's feet in Carol's lap, the two of them huddled on the couch under a blanket. Sophie adjusted to the loss of her tablet after a few days, and no longer asked for her mother to help find it. Even so, Carol sometimes heard her searching the drawers in the kitchen in the late afternoons when she was trying to sleep. Sophie probably suspected that her mother had hidden it away, but she hadn't said so.

"Mommy," Sophie said in her sweetest, most hopeful voice, "can we please get more kays?"

She had waited until the commercial in order to have her mother's full attention. Carol set her pen and her spiral notebook aside to brush the curls away from Sophie's hopeful brown eyes. "No. I'm sorry, sweetie, but we can't."

Sophie's lip trembled, but she bit down on it and turned back to the TV. By now she knew better than to argue the point. She also knew that she would find a way to ask it again when the moment seemed right, just as she had at least a dozen times before. Carol had learned quickly what "more kays" meant. There was no way to avoid knowing about it, because the message was the same in every episode.

"Tell your parents to let you watch us in 4K on a UHD TV!" Listabell would translate for Mister Mudgett while the fuzzy tyrant leaned in close over her shoulder. "The Toyman's coming soon, and you'll need to see all the colors to find the Numblycrumbs before he gets here!"

Carol had assumed at first that it was just a commercial, even though they never mentioned any brand names. Of course, her regular sources on the internet insisted that the show was different when you watched it on a high-resolution monitor like a 4K television. A cadre of convincing die-hards pointed out intricate patterns in the show's striped set pieces, and how, if the light hit them just right, those same patterns, like strange hieroglyphs, could be seen in the costumes themselves. They posted clips and screenshots that seemed to show odd outlines in the shapes of people, lurking at the edge of the frame. Carol had gone so far as to buy a new high-resolution laptop, plundering the emergency fund almost all the way down to nothing, just so she could see for herself.

And they were right. There were patterns in the backgrounds, on the costumes, everywhere. Straight lines arranged in starburst sigils, angles and whorls like some lost and ancient alphabet. The longer she stared at them, the more she began to think that she could start to understand what they meant. She found clips of Gib's conversion and watched them over and over. When she looked hard enough, she was sure she could see something standing behind him, its hands closing around his throat.

Sophie giggled as Mister Mudgett kicked Narly and sent him sprawling to the studio floor. At least, it had the appearance of a kick, as she could see no feet beneath the hat-to-floor tangle of yarn. There were those online who said that it wasn't yarn at all, that they had seen it move all on its own. They were the same people who speculated that Mister Mudgett might not be a costume at all.

The show had made a sharp decline in the past weeks, dropping all pretense of a coherent story and letting the characters run amok like unsupervised toddlers. Sophie seemed to almost prefer it this way, leaning forward as she watched, as if by getting closer she could make herself a part of it. Only when there was a commercial break—no clean wrap-ups now, just rough cuts away from the chaos—did she even seem to blink. Carol's foot twitched as she drummed her pen against the pages of the spiral notebook. She wondered what the show was doing to her daughter. She wondered what it was doing to both of them.

Narly tried to stand but Mudgett lashed out so hard that it knocked the top hat from his own head. Sophie laughed. Narly croaked back at Mudgett in that terrible almost-speech. Whatever it was that had changed Gib had changed him too. He hadn't even been on screen when it happened.

From the kitchen came the hollow ring of knuckles on the metal screen door. The kid was early, not supposed to be here for at least another forty minutes. The TV went dark, and faded in on a long shot of the stage, a fixed camera set in the distance that had become the last window into the Stumbly-bums' world. Listabell was on her back. Gib and Narly each had hold of one foot as they dragged her around the floor. Their costumes were all dirty and they were beginning to tear.

Carol looked down at her phone and thought that she could text him and tell him to come back later. Or better still, that he should leave the pills in the mailbox next to the door and she'd settle up with him later. Would he even agree to something like that? Carol didn't think that he would, and she didn't have the money to pay him anyway. She'd burned the emergency fund down to nothing buying the new computer and the bank account was scarcely any better. But she was down to her last four pills, even when she counted the one she kept separate because it had rolled behind the toilet, and four would barely carry her through to tomorrow.

The knocking came again, more urgent this time. Carol bit her lip. Mudgett had wandered into the corner of the frame and she could feel a voyeuristic thrill rising inside her, a fear that if she were to look away she would miss something important, maybe even critical. Her phone buzzed. The kid knew she was home. She drummed the pencil against the notepad. Mudgett stopped moving and stood frozen like a mannequin in his corner. It was probably safe for her to leave, and she would only be a minute. If she missed anything, she could watch it online in less than an hour. She thought she could wait that long if she had to.

The knocking came a third time and Carol sprang to her feet. She ran a hand through her hair, brushing it back from her eyes as she rushed into the kitchen. The kid watched her through the screen door, smiling appreciatively in that guileless way that he had. It made Carol smile too, and arch her back ever so slightly as she threw open the door.

"Yeah, hey, sorry about that," she said, leaning close. "I had the TV up in the other room. And I thought you weren't coming until two-thirty."

"Yeah, but I have to go be in Brixton for this thing with my family, and I figured you were usually home anyway, so..." His eyes wandered over her breasts, braless beneath her t-shirt, down to the subtle curve of her hips. He caught himself, but not before Carol caught him too.

"Anyway," he said fishing in his pocket for the little plastic bag, "I brought thirty. If you need more, I can come back tomorrow. No big deal."

"About that." Carol smiled what she hoped was her best smile. "I'm a little short right now. Just 'til the end of the week when my check comes in. You know how it is. So, I was thinking if it's okay, you could cover me until Friday?"

The kid's shoulders drooped. Carol added quickly, "I'm good for it. I promise."

"Yeah, it's just that..." The kid squinted and shuffled his foot. "I did that once with a guy at school, let him buy on credit. He left me hanging. Not that I think that you'd do that, too. It's just that, well, it's kind of a policy now. You know how it is."

Carol's jaw tightened. Sophie's laughter carried over from the other room, and it made her wonder what she was missing. "Yeah," she said quietly. "I know how it is."

"I could come back Friday," he said brightly. "I'll bring more then, too. Just tell me how many you need." But Friday was a world away. Friday might as well be on the other side of the moon.

She stepped toward him, mustering her courage, and let the screen door close behind her. "Or, you know, maybe..." She laid a hand on his arm that he didn't refuse. "I was thinking that maybe you could help me out? You know, just this once?"

The words felt stupid in her mouth, and a part of her hated herself for saying them. But she saw the eager look in the kid's eyes and knew that they would work. She took him by the hand and pulled him inside without having to say any more.

They passed by Sophie on the way to the bedroom, and he hesitated. She had moved to the floor, so close to the TV that her face almost touched it. She hadn't seen them come in, and the show was almost over.

"It's okay," Carol told him and brought him in the rest of the way. "Just wait here a sec." She rummaged beneath the mattress and left him unbuttoning his shirt. When she went to Sophie, it was with her hands held behind her back.

"Check it out, sweetie," she said as she held out the tablet with both hands. "Look what I found."

"I hate you!"

"Sweetie—"

Sophie stood on tiptoes, fists balled at her sides, her face red. "I hate you I hate you I hate you!"

Carol folded her arms across her chest. She felt sick to her stomach, but she knew that if she gave any ground now she'd lose the last bit of resolve she had. "There are lots of other shows. You can watch whatever you want, just not—"

"I don't want other shows. I want the Stumblybums! I want to see the Toyman! I want to see all the colors!" Sophie growled the words, trying to sound fierce. The absurdity of it threatened to uncork a spate of unwanted laughter and Carol bit down hard on her tongue to keep it back. She wanted to run to her room and curl away on the bed. The pills wore off quicker now, and she knew it would take at least three to quiet the nervous ache in her stomach. She wanted to flee and come back when the drugs had done their work, when she was able to think straight.

"I can't let you watch that show anymore, sweetie." She was using her reasonable mom voice, but even so, she heard the cracks in it. "It's not good for you. It's not good for either of us." The show was barely a show at all now. The characters didn't talk. They just muttered to each other in that weird almost-language. They still buzzed with activity, but the activity made no sense. Fans online tried to analyze their patterns, insisting that every exaggerated movement, every halting shuffle of feet, was building toward something, maybe something big. To Carol it seemed like nonsense, the pointless dancing of lunatics in an asylum. And yet, when she closed her eyes, all she could see was that faded, shifting outline, that Numblycrumb, with its hands around Gib's throat.

"I want daddy back. Daddy would let me watch Stumblybums all day long!"

"Well, if you can find him, you can ask him. How's that?" She regretted the words as soon as they'd left her mouth, but Sophie's screaming was like a knife in her brain and she was having trouble thinking straight.

Sophie growled in frustration, stomped to the couch and scooped up her tablet. She pushed at it with her thumbs, adding fresh smears to the fingerprints on the screen. She only paused to glare up at her mother. She was only five, but she knew how parental controls worked. Carol had blocked every Stumblybums site she knew, and she knew many. She'd unplugged the TV and hid the power cord, too. It was as much for herself as it was for Sophie. She had tried to stop watching, but kept peeking back late at night when Sophie was sleeping. There was something in the Stumblybums' halting, jerking dance that felt like a promise, like something new just waiting to be born, and it terrified her.

"Sweetie, that show..." Her stomach clenched. The little bag was on the shelf above the sink and it called out to her. "We'll watch whatever else you want. I'll watch it with you, ok? We can—"

"I don't want another show! I want the Toyman! I want Mister Mudgett! You're the worst mommy!"

Three pills to get through tonight. Two more tomorrow. Her daughter wasn't wrong.

Sophie straightened her back, her arms straight as steel, her fists balled tight. "You're the worst mommy and I hate you."

Carol closed her eyes. Her temples were throbbing and her stomach would not stay still. "Sweetie, I know you don't mean that."

"I hate you I hate you I hate you!"

"Well, I hate you too!"

The air grew still, and silence descended over them until all Carol could hear was the sound of her pulse hammering in her ears. Sophie's eyes were wide, and Carol could see the tears beginning to form in their corners. She wanted to scoop

Sophie into her arms and hold her close, but she could not make herself move.

Sophie's eyes spilled over with the dawning realization that something fundamental had changed between them, even though she didn't understand what it was. The look was gone in an instant, boiling over into a white-hot rage.

"I hate you." Sophie's voice was quiet, little more than a whisper. She blinked and more tears spilled from her eyes. The tablet fell from her hand and she ran. Carol wanted to stop her, but she didn't. When the bedroom door slammed, she was already on her way to the kitchen.

She held the little bag over the sink, turning it over, watching the six pills rolling inside, listening to them rattle against the plastic. Three tonight. Two more tomorrow. Her stomach flipped and churned at the thought, growling low. The sound of it made her think of Mister Mudgett, of the low and guttural chants that he sang as the Stumblybums danced.

She turned the bag upside-down and listened to the pills rattle as they fell down the drain.

Carol woke to the distant sound of a police siren, swung her feet off the bed, and waited for the world to stop spinning. Her mouth was dry and tasted of metal. Her limbs felt heavy and they did not want to move.

The kid lay sleeping next to her, half covered in the sheet. She didn't remember calling him, but he had shown up just the same. He'd brought something new with him this time, chalky little circles that burst like fireworks against the backs of her eyes. She told herself that she hadn't wanted to take them, but she knew that was a lie. She'd been shaking almost nonstop since she had flushed the little blue-and-whites and would have given anything just to feel right again. She hadn't even asked him what they would cost.

The siren faded off into the distance, and she wobbled a bit as she stood. Everything kept tilting and the air smelled sharp, like rain after a lightning strike. When she was sure she wasn't going to fall, she scooped a shirt from the floor and shrugged it on. It was too big, and covered her almost to her knees. It was Shaun's shirt and she wished, not for the first time, that it was him lying in the bed instead of this kid who could pass for her little brother. She looked at his feet, at the absurd way they hung off the edge of the bed, and wondered how long she'd have to wait before she kicked him out. She looked at the clock. It read 12:43. The Stumblybums had already started.

She thought of Sophie fuming in her room. She could fume all she wanted as long as she wasn't watching that damn show anymore. The thought of seeing Mister Mudgett again, with his matte of purple yarn that seemed to move on its own, sent a shudder across Carol's shoulder blades. And yet, she knew that she couldn't help herself. She would watch, and she would see him again, once Sophie went to sleep, if not before.

The kid shifted, snoring softly. She'd wake him in a minute, find a way to get him out of the house without Sophie seeing. But first she needed something to drive the dryness from her mouth. As she padded toward the kitchen she heard raised voices coming from the street outside, but couldn't make out the words. There was barely any light coming in through the windows, and it made her wonder if it was about to storm.

Then she heard Sophie giggle, and she froze in her steps.

The sound had come from the kitchen, from the table where she'd left the rest of the chalky white pills, where she'd left the laptop open when she'd taken the kid to bed with her.

Sophie giggled again, high and shrill. Beneath it was the sound of a caliope, random notes, fast and frantic, like a cat running over the keys.

"It's okay, Mommy," Sophie said. "The Numblycrumbs took away all my wrongthoughts, so everything's gonna be better now."

Carol crept around the corner, feeling her heartbeat quicken with every step. Sophie sat at the table, silhouetted in the glow of the laptop. On the screen in front of her, Mister Mudgett stood stock-still, filling the frame. Though the room was dark, Carol could see vague shapes moving in the shadows beyond the screen, their outlines barely visible. One of them reached out and put a hand on Sophie's shoulder.

Sophie giggled again, the mad cackling of a jungle bird. From somewhere out in the distance came screams and the low rumble of an explosion. The sky beyond the screen door roiled and writhed, not with clouds, but with something that looked like strands of yarn.

Sophie turned in her chair, and looked up at Carol with wide eyes that were no longer her own. "The Toyman's here, Mommy," she said in a hoarse croak before her voice was lost to babbling. "He showed me all the colors, Mommy. I can see them! I can see them all!"

Shadowman

THEY CAME AT HIM out of the setting sun like fighter planes, riding low over the handlebars, legs pumping the pedals like little propellers. Yasha saw them too late, and by the time he turned his bike around, shuffling it through the turn between shaking legs, they were on him. They took turns shoving, three against one, until he finally went down hard, scraping along the blacktop in a tangle of limbs and spinning metal.

They were at the edge of the grassy field that sat next to the school, at the corner where the big boulder loomed, taller than Yasha, taller than all of them. School ground had always meant safety before, but whatever unwritten rule had kept Cody and his jeering cohort at bay was no longer in force. They spread out around him, leaving Yasha no option but to scramble up the sloping face of the boulder on all fours until he stood looking down at the three of them, panting with exertion and fear.

Pinning him at the boulder had been a miscalculation. Yasha could read that much in the confusion on their faces as they squinted up at him, their eyes darting to Cody, waiting for his next move. The wheels behind Cody's eyes were turning. No doubt he was measuring how long it would take for him to get to the top of the boulder, and whether Yasha might kick out and send him back down before he ever made it up. He probably had an inkling that Yasha wouldn't try it, not if it meant he might get dragged back down in the process, but he couldn't be sure. It was only an instant before the wheels grew still, and a lopsided grin spread across Cody's face.

"Yasha, Yasha, is a girl. Dumbest girl in the whole world!"

He said it in a little sing-song, and though Yasha had heard it a hundred times before, it still brought a flush of shame to his cheeks. The other two joined in on the next go-around, their voices high and mocking as they squinted up at him and rocked their heads in time with the words. The sun was at Yasha's back, and he was grateful for it because it meant that they could only see him in silhouette. It meant that they couldn't see the tears running down his face.

"What's the matter, little girl?" Weese called up to him when they'd grown tired of the song. "Can't you come down and play?"

"Yeah, little girl." Malloy said. "You left your bike. Wouldn't want anything to happen to it."

"Nah," Cody said after a little thought. "If she comes down here, we'll just have to smell her." He scrunched up his face in a parody of disgust and shook his head like there was something foul just under his nose.

"Yasha smells like onions! Yasha smells like onions!"

"Shut up!" Yasha wished that his voice hadn't sounded so high and desperate, so on the verge of breaking into sobs. But it was enough to stop their sing-song chanting, if only for a moment. In the silence, he could feel the blood oozing from his knee, pooling in the folds of his sock. He could see the long shadow of his body, its limbs thick, its middle wide, stretching out to fall at Malloy's feet.

It was Cody who broke the quiet with a laugh that burst out of his mouth like a shook-up soda can. As one, the three threw his words back at him with a mocking lilt. "Shut up! Shut up! Shut up!"

"Just leave me alone!"

"Come down and make us, onion girl," Weese said, his close-cropped blond hair glinting like tiny nails in the setting sun.

"I'm not a girl!"

Weese spit the words back at him, but Cody seemed to think it over. "Maybe he's not a girl," he said. "Maybe he's just some... thing."

"Yeah," Malloy said. "Trailer trash is just trash. It belongs in a dumpster."

"There's a dumpster right over there behind the school," Weese said, cocking his head toward the building. "Maybe we need to get him down and throw him in."

"Be doing everyone a favor," Malloy said.

Cody seemed to think it over. "Nah," he said at last. "Don't want to touch him. Who knows what diseases he's got."

"Trailer trash disease," Weese said, nodding. "Don't want to get any on you."

"Don't let him touch you," Malloy said. "He'll make you poor too."

Yasha balled his fists around his thumbs and bit down hard on his lip to stop the tears. He wanted to leap from the rock and right onto Malloy's head. He wanted to punch him right in the nose, hear it crack beneath his fist. He wanted to pin him down and keep hitting until the teeth flew from his mouth. But he knew that, whatever he did to Malloy the others would do back to him, and worse, assuming that he managed to do anything at all. He'd never hit anyone. Not once, no matter how many times they'd chased him, no matter how many times they'd pushed him to the ground.

"Don't be stupid," Weese said. "You can't *give* somebody poor. It's not catching. It's, like, something you're born with."

"I know that!" Malloy squared off against him, keyed up and ready for a fight. "I'm just sayin' you don't want to touch him, is all."

His shadow trailed off behind him, but Yasha's shadow was bigger, so big that if he shifted his position it would dwarf Malloy entirely. If his shadow were a man, it would have no problem punching Malloy into the ground. It might even be able to take on all three of them.

"This is dumb," Cody said, with an air of finality. Whenever he said it like that, it was a sure sign that he was getting bored with his torments. Yasha felt the tingle in his spine ease a little. "Come on. Let's leave the trash to his trash pile."

"Yeah," Weese echoed. "Leave the trash to his trash pile."

Together, they began to angle their bikes around. Yasha felt his body unclench, and saw the unclenching reflected in his shadow on the ground. Malloy must have seen it too, because he paused halfway and looked down at Yasha's bike laying on its side in the dirt. A grim smile crept across his face and Yasha's shadow tensed again. Malloy pushed off from his handlebars and brought his foot down on the other bike's wheel. The spokes bent beneath his weight, and the tire popped loose as the rim bent sideways.

Malloy stared down at what he'd done, surprised and more than a little proud, his eyes wide, his mouth pulled into a little smirking O. The others stared with him, the energy crackling between them over this new transgression, this escalation in their torments. Yasha trembled as he looked down at the damaged wheel, this wound that would not heal the way the bruises they had given him had healed, the way his bloody knee would heal. They had ruined it, ruined him, in a way that he could not fix.

The air grew silent as the four of them stared, all eyes fixed on the broken wheel, all their breath held in their chests. It was Cody who broke that silence. He let out a long, spitting laugh between pursed lips, doubling over as if Malloy's foot on the broken wheel was the funniest thing he'd ever seen. It gave the others permission to join in, and absolved them of their crime in the name of the pleasure it had given them. Yasha felt hot shame creep its way up his neck and into his cheeks. His rage grew, coiling in his gut like a pail full of snakes. He felt his arm rising, unbidden, and watched his shadow-arm rise with it, rising up Malloy's legs and across his body until its hand found Malloy's throat.

Malloy grew silent again as he looked up at Yasha, standing on the boulder with the sun at his back, then down again at the shadow that had been made to fall upon him. He squinted, confused, as the others stopped laughing, not knowing what to make of this new development, this strange act of defiance. Yasha held the shadow-hand to Malloy's neck, watched it squeeze its fingers in time with his own. Malloy burst out laughing again and the others followed his lead.

"Freak," he said, and worked up a mouthful of spit to launch down at the broken bicycle. Still, he took care to wheel himself out of reach of that shadow before he turned himself the rest of the way around.

The others each paused in turn to spit on the ruins of Yasha's bike. Then they rode away, standing high on their pedals, legs pumping, not looking back. Yasha could hear them long after they were gone, their high laughter calling back to him on the wind, relentless and indifferent.

———— ◆◇◆ ————

Yasha sat on the rock until well after the sun went down, afraid that they might turn back for him, afraid of what Grandmother would say when she saw the ruins of his bicycle, when he showed up outside the trailer door, battered and bloody. He bent the wheel back into shape as best he could and walked it along, limping, until the cracked pavement gave way to gravel, and the light beneath a dozen low rooftops lent a warm glow to the darkening sky.

"Is my name a girl's name?" he asked Grandmother, after the hot soup had warmed his insides and she sat before him, water and cloth in a tin pan to clean his wounds.

"Of course not," Grandmother said, her voice rough like sandpaper. "Why do you ask such a foolish question?"

"They say my name's a girl's name."

"Who is this that says such nonsense?"

"Everybody."

She let out a coarse sound of disapproval and dug the cloth into the scratches on his knees, hard enough to make him wince.

"No," Grandmother said. "Yasha is not a name for girl."

As she spoke, her words brought with them the sound of the old country, filling the air like the smoke from her cigarettes, rough and enveloping, but sweet all the same. It was a world that Yasha had never seen, but a world that seemed to live all around them in the tiny space the two of them called home, from the fragrant herbs hung to dry in the kitchen window to the deep red cushions that smelled of age and spice and far-away. It was a world, Yasha knew, where boys could pedal their bikes without looking over their shoulder, where his enemies would not ride him down, but turn and run when they saw him coming.

"Yasha is a strong name," she told him. "A *proud* name. It is name for princes, for great leaders of men. It is old name, as old as our people, as old as the hills where we came from. Probably older still. Is a good name. Is even better because it is *your* name."

He thought about this as the warm water trickled down his legs and washed the blood away. "I wish I was strong" he said into his chest.

Grandmother opened her mouth to speak, but turned away, coughing. Something wet was loose in her chest, and when she spoke again the sound of it was in her voice. "You cannot help that these boys torment you," she said. "They see weakness, and it draws them like the sweat draws little biting flies."

The words should have stung, but there was a tenderness in her eyes that did not so much as hint at pity. "But you cannot help this. After all, you are your father's child."

She pressed her hand to his cheek. It was bony and rough with calluses and he leaned into it.

"But it was your mother who gave you this name. Mothers always know the right names of their children. They know it in their hearts before they are even born. She gave you this name because she knew what was in *your* heart. The heart of a warrior. A heart that beats with the blood of all our people."

Yasha closed his eyes. He tried to listen for the sound of his heart, but it was fleeting and faint and barely there at all. He wanted to tell this to Grandmother, if only to hear her tell him he was wrong, but she was already pushing herself up to stand on trembling legs.

"It is late," she said as she shuffled toward the curtain that hid the back of the little trailer where she slept. "Enough nonsense for tonight, no?"

She squeezed her hand down on his shoulder as she passed and yanked the curtain closed behind her. Yasha patted his legs dry and emptied the tin plate into the crowded sink before he stripped down to his underpants and burrowed under the blankets on the little sofa beneath the window. He looked at the wall, at the shadows cast by the swaying trees outside, and

let the sounds of Grandmother's snoring lull him into a deep
sleep.

The hollow banging on the aluminum screen door woke him,
but Grandmother was already shuffling toward the sound,
bare-footed in her threadworn housecoat.

"Is this the place where Yasha lives?" asked a voice when
Grandmother opened the door. It was a woman's voice, trembling and strained. "Are you his mother?"

"He is my grandson," Grandmother said, hand to her back
as she straightened.

"Is he home?"

"What does it matter?"

"It matters," the voice said, rising, "because I want him to
come out here and see what he did to my son."

Yasha kept the blanket up to his chin, barely daring to move.
He hoped that Grandmother wouldn't call to him to come
out, because he was still only dressed in his underpants and he
didn't recognize this voice on the other side of the door. He
didn't like the way she'd said *place*, spitting it out as if the little
trailer—his home—were beneath her contempt. Still, he crept
to the edge of the couch, craning to see past Grandmother and
out into the bright space beyond.

Malloy was there, standing just on the other side of the
threshold, smaller than he remembered, staring down at the
little patch of dirt between his feet. Yasha could not see the
woman who had her fingers gripped tight to his shoulder, but

the bruises on his neck were unmistakable. They stood out, bright purple against his pale skin, their edges fading to yellow.

Grandmother regarded them with her lips pressed tight and called back to him. "Yasha, did you do this to this boy?"

"No, Grandmother," he said, but he had to work to keep the question out of his voice. The bruises were long and they stood out as clear as fingerprints, the mark of a hand where his shadow had touched Malloy's neck.

"Tell the truth," she said, fixing him with narrowed eyes. "If you lie, I will know. Did you do this?"

"No, Grandmother."

She stared at him a moment longer before she nodded and turned back to the woman he could not see. "There," she said. "The boy has said he did not do this. So he did not do this."

"And you're just going to, what? Just believe him? Just like that?" The unseen woman's voice was rising, her hand on Malloy's shoulder, squeezing tighter.

"Grandmother shrugged. "Yasha is good boy. He does not lie. Not to me."

Yasha felt a sudden pain at that, worse than any pain that Malloy had ever inflicted on him. He wanted to leap from the couch and tell Grandmother everything, but he only cowered beneath the blanket.

"So you're telling me that *my* son is lying, is that it?" The woman's voice was shrill now, almost monstrous.

"I do not know what your son has said. How can I call him a liar?"

"He said that your boy did this to him." Malloy rocked and stumbled as his mother pulled him off balance. "He put his hands on *my son's* throat and choked him!"

Malloy squinted up at her and tried to pull away. "That's not what I—"

"He said that he *attacked* him. You see the bruises. How else would he get bruises like that?"

Grandmother considered. She took Malloy's chin in her hand and lifted it as he tried to squirm away. He seemed so small now, diminished to the point where he was no longer the same kid who had chased him down and stomped on his bicycle. He no longer seemed capable, this little boy who withered now beneath Grandmother's steady gaze, like a bug beneath a magnifying glass.

"Yasha, did you do as this woman says?"

"No, Grandmother." Yasha was grateful for the way she'd phrased the question, that she had not asked him if he had given Malloy those bruises. What would he have told her then? That he had wanted to hurt Malloy, that he had wanted to hurt him and all the others? That he had wanted to over and over again, through all the months of torment, that he had wanted every hurt they had inflicted on him returned to them, magnified and all at once? That maybe, after all this time, he'd finally found the means to do that, to do all of that? That his shadow had done it, just because he'd thought about it? That maybe his shadow could do it again, no matter that he didn't understand how?

Grandmother let go of Malloy's chin and he pulled away, wincing. "It is settled," she said. "You can go now."

The woman behind the door stepped forward. Yasha saw her clearly for the first time, her hair neat and sprayed, her fists balled, her dress crisp and expensive-looking. She pushed past Malloy and he cowered behind her, barely an afterthought.

"No, it is certainly not settled. And *how dare you* put your filthy hands on my son?"

"My hands are clean," Grandmother said. "Can your boy say the same?"

"And what is *that* supposed to mean?"

Grandmother sighed. "All my life, I see boys like this one," she said. "Boys push. Boys fight. Boys sometimes go too far, and this is okay. This is what boys do."

She was no longer talking to the mother. She was talking to Malloy, staring right at him as he peeked out around his mother's body, and he withered beneath Grandmother's gaze.

"But this boy... I have seen this boy, and I have seen what he does. I know the look in his eye. He sees what men do, and he picks the worst of those things for himself. Worse, he enjoys such things, more and more, each time he gets away with them. He is like a tree with too many crawling mites digging in under the bark. He needs a gardener to prune him back so he can grow straight. Grow tall."

Here she raised her gaze to Malloy's mother, who had opened her mouth to speak but seemed to forget her words the moment Grandmother's eyes met hers. The woman's lips moved in a little O, like a fish gasping for air.

"No child should be left to grow as this one has," Grandmother said. "It is not too late, not yet, but it will be. And soon,

I think. I cannot tell you what to do, but I can tell you that I will not let my Yasha become like this one."

The mother's face was turning redder by degrees. "How *dare* you?" she spat. "How dare you presume to tell me how to raise my child? You, in this filthy little place with your *filthy* little boy!" She tried to say more, but Grandmother was already shutting the door, and whatever words Malloy's mother had left became muffled, then died away completely. The last thing Yasha saw as the door closed was Malloy's face, cringing and chastened, and Yasha could not help but smile.

Grandmother stood with her hand on the door handle. Outside, Yasha could hear Malloy's mother ranting at her son, the shuffle of his feet dragging in the dirt as they moved away. When he could hear it no more, Grandmother convulsed, and a great fit of coughing worked its way up through her back and out her throat. On and on it went, until her face turned red and Yasha began to fear that she might never breathe again. He forgot the blanket, forgot that he was only in his underpants, and went to her side to steady her. She only waved him away.

When it was done, the air in the little trailer seemed darker somehow, Grandmother shrunken and diminished. Steadying herself on the door handle, she breathed, and her breath crackled in her chest like tiny fireworks. Yasha listened to it, edging closer, wondering not for the first time what he might do if Grandmother fell to the floor. Who would he call? Who would come? It was only the two of them in this tiny tin box that seemed so much smaller now than it ever had before. There was no one who would help them. There was only Grandmother. Grandmother, and himself.

He pressed his hand to Grandmother's shoulder and she spun on him. She found his ear and pinched down on it with her thumb, lifting him. He cried out and stumbled forward, struggling to stay on his feet as Grandmother's grip tightened. He stood on tiptoes as she lowered her face to his own, close enough that he could smell her breath, thick and sour, like vegetables left out in the sun.

"What would your mother say, hm?" Her voice was still hoarse, barely more than a whisper. "To use these gifts this way? To waste them on petty nonsense like a child. Like worse than a child?"

She looked down at him, looked into him, and though he wanted to squirm away he was too frightened to do anything but stand his ground. "Use what has been given to you," she said, her voice softer now, sharing a secret. "But use it as a man. Do not use it as a boy. Be your mother's son, always. Do you understand?"

Her grip tightened. The pain was so fierce that the edges of his vision began to darken. Still, he could see the tears welling in her eyes, the flecks of blood at the corners of her mouth.

"Yes! Yes, Grandmother," he cried.

She let go of him then. Diminished once more, she turned her head to let loose a single wet cough to clear her throat. When she turned back, her eyes had become kind again, and Yasha could see something in them that looked like regret. She reached out to him, and though he shied away, she cupped his cheek gently in her hand. It felt cool against his skin as she thumbed his hot tears away.

"You are a good boy, Yasha," she said. "One day, you will be a good man. You *must* be a good man."

"Yes, Grandmother," he said, and though he did not understand he knew that he would try, if only to keep her from seizing his ear again, if only to keep her horrible coughing at bay.

Grandmother nodded, satisfied. All traces of her earlier ferocity were gone, and she was simply Grandmother again. The wet sound in her chest had faded, and as she patted his cheek, the edges of her mouth curled ever so slightly upward. It was as if she was seeing something more in him than just himself, as if she was seeing through time to a place that she, and only she could only glimpse. She smiled, as if what she saw there was enough.

Without another word, she shuffled away and closed the threadbare curtain behind her, leaving Yasha alone. He dressed in the dark and in silence, listening all the while for the sounds of Grandmother on the other side of the curtain, holding his breath, not daring to make a sound until her ragged breathing gave way to soft and peaceful snores.

<hr>

Grasshoppers scattered at Yasha's feet as he kicked his way through the tall grass. He chased them, taking care to avoid the stalks of spiky seeds that always snagged onto his socks, and when he caught them he held them clasped between his hands until they spit brown ichor onto his palm and he let them fly away. All the while, his shadow led the way before him, diminished though it was by the noontime sun. He watched its movements, half-expecting at any moment for it pull free from his feet and start to move on its own.

He held out his hand, and his shadow found a fat grasshopper clinging to a sagging stalk of grass. He tried to flick it from its perch with his shadow's fingers, but it would not move. He closed it in his shadow's fist and squeezed until the thing became bored and hopped away, drifting down on fluttering wings to vanish out of sight. Still, Yasha smiled, for he had seen the bruises on Malloy's throat and could picture them still: four angry patches where the shadow had left its mark. What's more, he could still picture Malloy standing with his head hung low, weak and hiding behind his mother, so diminished that he was hardly worth thinking about at all.

The high sun fell hot upon Yasha's shoulders and left his mouth feeling as dry as the cracked earth beneath his feet. Soon the summer would give way to fall, and to the low sun of winter, when the shadows grew longest of all. They would fear him then, these boys who chased and bloodied him. Not one of them would be beyond his reach. But even as he pictured his shadow falling across their frightened faces, he could hear Grandmother's words echo behind every thought. He would be a good man, he told himself, but he would never again allow himself to suffer the bad ones.

He picked his way down the packed-earth slope that led to the edge of the little creek. There, he cupped water into his mouth and watched little tadpoles scatter as the moving surface of the stream dappled in the sunlight. He could see his shadow shimmering and dancing with them along the bottom, so much more alive than even his own reflection. Life moved, and his shadow moved with it. He lost himself in the motion, and did not notice when two new shadows slid up behind him.

At once Yasha's face was under the water, hands at the back of his neck holding him down as he tried to scream. The surface of the water roiled, and all he could see was mud as he thrashed and tried to break free. He swallowed water, and when at last he felt as if his lungs would give out, they hauled him back and threw him down onto the bank.

"What did you do to Malloy?" Weese's face was red, his fists balled. Without giving him time to answer he grabbed Yasha by the shirt and tried to pull him up, but the shirt tore and Yasha fell back down. "What did you do to him, you freak?"

Cody stood behind him, wiping his wet hands on his shirt, his face screwed up in disgust like he'd just put his hands in something awful. "Put some kind of spell on him," he said. "Him and his crazy witch grandmother."

At the mention of his grandmother, Yasha shot to his feet, fists balled at his sides. Cody's eyes danced with eager amusement, but Weese was so scrunched and red-faced that Yasha could almost believe he was crying.

"They won't answer the door." Weese was near screaming, his words thick with snot. "There was an ambulance in his driveway. They wheeled him out with an oxygen mask over his face and they took him away. What did you do to him? What did you do!"

Yasha's shadow was behind him now, but the shadows of the other two boys were drawing closer. "How'd you do it, little trash girl?" Cody asked, still as cool as if he was asking him the time. "Little freak. Tell us how you did it and we might even let you go."

Yasha watched their shadows moving on the ground. The sun was in his eyes but he could still see the raw panic on Weese's face, the promise of violence in Cody's smile. If only he could circle around behind them, get the sun in their eyes, his shadow across their throats, but they had him trapped against the riverbank, unable to move.

"They wouldn't tell me what happened!" Weese's cheeks were wet and Yasha knew now that it wasn't from the river. "Did you kill him? Just tell me you didn't kill him."

"Nah," Cody said quietly. "He didn't kill him. He's too much of a pussy to kill him. He's too much of a pussy to even fight back. Isn't that right?"

Weese took a long look at Cody's narrow smile and wiped his face with the back of his hand. He sniffed and said, "Yeah. Yeah, that's right."

Cody's smile became sly and hungry. "You're not going to fight back, are you, little trash girl?" he asked as he stepped closer. "Too bad. It'll be more fun if you do."

They fell on him then. Yasha did fight back, for a while, until Weese pinned his arms and Cody sat on his legs and there was no fight left in him. But Yasha still smiled a little, just before the world went dark. He had seen the hesitation in Weese's eyes as he came on. He had seen how careful he was not to step in Yasha's shadow.

By the time Yasha awoke on the river bank, night had fallen. He lay there a while, taking inventory, moving his body by degrees, making sure that nothing was broken, making sure that everything still worked. Everything did not. His face had swollen on one side and would not let him see out of that eye. His teeth were all there, but they felt loose against the puffy flesh of his cheek. Something in his chest stabbed as he righted himself. He did not think his wrist was broken, but it still screamed when he used it to push himself up off the ground.

Weary and stumbling, he walked the long way back home, keeping to the dirt paths that only he and the other children knew. He kept his head down as he crossed the big road, not wanting to see his shadow in the glow of the street lamps, hunch-backed and shuffling and useless. And yet, when he moved into the darkness again, he felt its loss, as if he had just discovered a new limb, only to have it hacked away.

He wondered what Grandmother would say when she saw him. He wondered which Grandmother it would be, the one who cleaned his wounds and fed him soup, or the one who cuffed his ears. He no longer knew which one he deserved. All he knew was that he wished she was there for him to hide behind, the way that Malloy had hidden behind his mother. He wondered if they'd been lying about the ambulance. He didn't think so. They'd meant to hurt him this time, really hurt him, and they'd succeeded. It was too far for a joke, but maybe not too far for revenge.

The lights were all off in the little trailer. The sky was full of clouds, the moon a pale glow behind them that barely gave enough light to see by. And yet, his bicycle seemed to shine with a light all its own. It had been propped next to the little metal steps so there'd be no missing it. The wheel had been bent back into place. Some of the spokes were missing, but apart from that it had been made whole again. Yasha breathed deep and felt the dull-knife stab of his ribs, his lips split and bloody as the night air moved over them. It would be the kind Grandmother, then. The thought made his pains worse somehow. He felt the chill breeze at his back, and realized that he could barely bring himself to open the door.

Inside, the air had gone cold and still. The little couch he used for a bed was still rumpled and unmade, and where there should have been the smell of something warm and rich coming from the pot on the little stove, there was only the dry smell of Grandmother's hanging herbs, the close scent of unwashed bedsheets.

He went to the gap in the frayed curtain and stood before it, holding his breath, listening for a sound, any sound, but it did not come. He waited for the rustling of the rounded shape beneath the blanket, the rhythm of faint snoring, but he knew he would not hear them again. He had felt the emptiness of the place, the absence, as soon as he stepped inside. He wiped back the tears that spilled from his swollen eye and didn't mind the pain. He preferred it to what he might find when he pushed the little curtain aside. There was nothing left for him there now, and as long as he did not see it, he could tell himself that it wasn't so.

Unsteady, he rode out into the night, bouncing along the dirt paths and gravel roads, testing his legs and finding strength in them that he hadn't realized was still there. It was only when he reached the paved streets that he finally allowed himself to cry, really cry the big, ugly tears that he'd been holding back since the thin metal door banged shut behind him. He blinked them away as the bike wobbled beneath him, knowing that he would never hear the sound of that door again, knowing that he would never again feel Grandmother's hand, rough and cool against his cheek.

Houses rose up out of the darkness by ones and twos. By the time they lined the street on either side, his tears had dried. His swollen eye had opened a little and he could see them clearly: the well-lit rooms beyond their windows, the pictures hung in their frames. They grew larger with each one he passed, crowding closer together behind iron fences, behind neatly manicured lawns. He saw the people inside, standing content-edly in the light with no thought of the darkness outside.

He knew the place he was looking for. He had ridden by it before in the daylight, like a moth flying too close to a fire, when he had wanted to see this place where his tormentor lived. It looked barely different now, lit with spotlights that shined up onto the bone-white siding, with lanterns set astride its heavy oak doors. Yasha veered into the circular driveway and let his bike fall behind him. He stared up at the darkened windows. He did not know how late it was, but he could almost picture Cody asleep in his bed, untroubled by the things he had done. He could see him there, smiling, secure in knowing he was safe in his home, where nothing could touch him.

Yasha thought of this as he stepped onto the lawn and put the spotlights at his back. He watched his shadow rise up the wall to fall across the window. He watched it as its arms rose up, stretching to cover the place from end to end, a monster-shaped hole in the light, a giant big enough to tear the whole house from its foundations. He smiled as the shadow spread its fingers wide, and squeezed.

Carpenter's Thumb

THERE WASN'T ANY PAIN, not at first, but I knew it was coming. That's the way it was with these things. It was never about the pain, but the long, slow anticipation of it, like skidding off a wet road into a wall you know you can't avoid. I looked down at my left thumb, at the metal nail the hammer had missed and the living one it hadn't, and knew that this would hurt like a sonofabitch.

On the other side of the roof peak, Carl must have heard my pounding stop, because his stopped, too. His spiky blond head popped up from behind it like a cork from underwater, and I could see that he was grinning. "What's the matter?" he asked, knowing full well what the matter was. "Did we have a little accident?"

That's when the pain hit me, spreading across the top of the thumb and down into the meat of it like it was trapped in a vise. I drew in a little hiss of air as spots appeared before my eyes and I felt my body start to pitch backward. The harness around my middle was there to take my weight, and I let it. Still, the pain spread out, thick and flat, catching hold and digging in.

Carl was laughing now in that needle-sharp way he had. The sound of hammers around me dropped away as, one by one, the others stopped their work and looked over at him, then at me. I brought the thumb to my mouth, sucking at it as if I could suck the pain right out of it. It had leveled off at a spot somewhere between dull ache and total agony. The jagged edge of the thumbnail scraped against my tongue, but compared to the rest, it barely registered.

"Awwww," Carl called out. "Did widdle baby hurt his widdle thumb? Does widdle baby want his bottle and his blankie?" Then he let loose with another hyena laugh and a convulsion that threw him back into his own harness. It took his weight, and not for the first time, I found myself wishing that it hadn't. In my mind, the nylon strap that held him there slid loose, and he went sailing to the pavement three stories down, that laugh trailing him the whole way.

Quinn was over on the other end of the slope, at the end of a long safety line, and he walked his way over toward me. Most of the others were already back at work, laying shingles over black paper, banging them down. "Can you move it?" he asked.

Reluctantly, I pulled the thumb from my mouth and took a look at it. Already a small crescent of purple blister was spreading its way out beneath the nail. I wiggled it a little. The pain didn't seem to get any worse.

"Well," he said, "it doesn't look broken, but it's a doozy all right. Take some time, and when you're ready get back on the hammer. We need to finish this peak up by nightfall." He started back toward the end of the roof, but not before shooting a warning glance in Carl's direction. The little guy kept his head down, eyes on the spot he was working on.

But as soon as Quinn was gone, I could hear him starting to giggle again.

———————

The next morning, the first thing I did was take inventory of the damage. Quinn was right; it was a doozy. Beneath the nail lay a football shape of reddish black. At its center was a pus-white core, split down the center with another splotch of black. The slightest pressure on it awoke new pain almost equal to the first, and always it ached with a low, persistent throb.

Quinn insisted on having another look at it before he would let me back up on the roof the next day. Not that he would have bothered if it were anyone else. Any man on the line who ever swung a hammer had had that bad or worse, but Quinn insisted all the same. It was just a pretense, but both of us knew better than to say anything about it. I held the thumb out to him, but as he judged it, I could see he was really judging me.

He had plenty of reason to. I'd been late three times that month, and even when I had been on time, I might as well have stayed home. These days it was taking me twice as long to finish off a row as it should have, and when it was done you could see the marks from where the nails went in wrong and the way that some of the shingles were just a little off kilter. Any other foreman would have kept me down the ladder, but Quinn was different. I would have said that it was because he was my friend, but I don't think anyone on the line could have called him that. I might have said that it was because he respected me, but lately I hadn't done anything to earn it. In the end, I suppose, it was just his way of being decent.

But his eyes were critical now as he looked from the thumb to my face and back to the thumb again. Those eyes caught everything up on the peaks, and they took in everything here. He noticed the ragged edge of the nail, bitten down until there was nothing left of the white to show. He saw the skin beneath it, chewed dead and peeling into little pale craters. He saw these things, but he didn't mention them, and for that I was grateful.

I had told him about Anna the second time I showed up late. I hadn't meant to, but I was tired, and still feeling the buzz from drinking the night before. I hadn't told him everything, though, because I hadn't needed to. Anna had a reputation before we met, and she lived up to it on the night I'd walked in on her. My mind kept replaying the scene as I opened the door and found the two of them there, moving together on top of the sheets, and every time that sight came to me, I'd take the nail in my teeth and start to gnaw.

Most of the guys on the line knew about Anna, too. Gossip like that was too good not to spread, and when it came to dirt the guys were worse than the ladies rotary. They kept quiet when I was around though, probably because they knew it could have just as easily happened to one of them. Carl kept quiet about it, too, but with him it was only because he was waiting for the right time to bring it up. Let the wounds start to close a little, then he'd get the needle out and tear them right back open.

How Carl had stayed on the line was anybody's guess. He was no friend of Quinn's, that much was sure. He'd taken the little pipsqueak to task about his antics on the peaks more than once. I'd expected Quinn to leave him down months ago, but still Carl kept turning up. Word went around once that Carl was the owner's nephew, and that Quinn had no choice but to keep him on, but no one really believed that the old man would run a crew where he couldn't pick his own men.

"You good to go up?" Quinn asked. His stern look carried the true meaning of the question.

"Yeah," I said, not really sure, but knowing it was what I had to say to get my place on the line. He looked at me for a while, sizing me up, but at the same time inviting me to say more, if saying more was what I wanted. But it wasn't what I wanted, and he seemed to understand.

"All right. Take your spot," he said finally. I turned and started off in the direction of the ladder. "But watch that thumb. You abuse that thing any more and its gonna want to get even."

He walked away, smiling at his joke, but something about it made me take another look at that thumbnail and the bruise that had welled up underneath. At once the shape of it caught me, and I noticed something that I hadn't seen before. It was something in the colors, the way the little swell of black cut through the milky stretch of white. Strange how I hadn't noticed it before, but now that I had, I could not see it as anything else. It was just a bruise, and yet, it looked like much more than a bruise.

It looked like an eye.

———◦———

July can be one of the worst months for roof work. The sun is always high, and the heat of it gets magnified against the black tar paper and asphalt shingles until working there you start to feel like a piece of meat on a griddle. Worse yet, there's no shade and nothing to do about it but pray for clouds to make the going a little bit easier. A boss like Quinn wouldn't even send a crew up on months like that unless he was behind and under a deadline that threatened to take a bonus out of our pockets.

Of course, that was just the kind of month we were having.

But it wasn't all bad. We got there early, and we went home early. We took our lunches groundside in the shade while the worst of the sun passed over. On the roof, everyone was miserable, which meant everyone was quiet. Without the constant chatter, it became easier for me to focus on my work. The endless repetition of shingle after shingle, nail after nail was like therapy to me. It seemed to shut out everything else: Anna, the drinking, the bouts of insomnia that left me dragging into work late most days. It all got pushed aside, and even though the heat was like torture, I began to feel better.

My accident with the hammer had helped too. The pain had forced me to focus, because I was willing to do anything to avoid going through it again. My first swings after that had been tentative, almost too careful, and in a way it was like starting from the beginning again. Gradually, I became more and more confident, like a machine resetting itself, and before long I was back to laying asphalt as fast as I had in the old days, before *she* came along. It was like I had taken something back from her, and I noticed that I was back to being myself. Quinn had noticed it, too.

Now the pain in the thumb was gone, but the evidence of it was still there in that little eye-shape in the middle of the nail. It had been two months, but the bruise was still as black and angry as ever. And though it didn't hurt anymore, there was still something about it that made me uneasy. The shape of it was so much like an eye, and there were times I could almost swear that it was staring it me. It seemed such a silly thought, one I would dismiss as soon as it came, but later I'd look down and see that black and purple pupil inside that field of yellow-white, and that unsettled feeling would come back over me. It was as if it was sitting there watching me, and it didn't like what it saw.

But maybe that was only because when I looked at myself, I didn't like what I saw, either.

Outwardly, I was fine. I was better than fine. I was in tip-top form again, first up the ladder and last one down. The heat didn't get to me, and it didn't break my stride. I was working steeper slopes and still getting them done quicker than anyone on the shallows. Any guy on that line would have thought I'd done a complete one-eighty, that I was once-and-for-all over her, and over every last insult and embarrassment she had put me through.

Only, I wasn't over her. In my heart, I wanted to kill her, and for that, I began to hate myself.

Sure, I'd fantasized about it before. The first time she'd come home at three-thirty in the morning—out with the girls, she'd said—I knew what she'd been up to. Being out with the girls wasn't what had smeared the makeup at the corners of her eyes, and it hadn't given her hair that rough, pillow-tossed look, either. I was no fool, and seeing her sneak back into our bedroom, I knew what she'd been up to. In the knowing, just for an instant, I'd wished she was dead.

But this was different. This time it was real, that murderous rage that welled up when I thought of her, and it wasn't going away. Her face was in front of me every time the blood beneath that thumbnail pulsed. I thought about her with each fresh throb of pain, and every time I could see that thumb squeezing its way down against her windpipe. Again and again the scene came to me and I would watch, thumb in my mouth, gnawing.

And there were nights, nights when I couldn't sleep and I found myself driving past the apartment where she lived.

"BOO!"

It was Carl. He had jumped up at me from the other side of the peak, his face twisted into something between anticipation and insane glee. He had caught me in mid-swing, too, with no time to recover. Even as the hammer came down, I could see where it was going to land. I could see it and there was nothing I could do but watch.

It came down, again, on top of the thumb.

This time, there was no waiting for the pain. I felt it, sharp and hard, the very moment of impact. More than that, this new pain seemed to awaken the old pain and multiply it, as if somehow that old pain had always been there, waiting for something to set it free.

And this time when the hammer hit, I heard something go crunch.

Carl took a second to register what had happened. In that moment, he hung there, his eyes wide and his mouth open, looking like a dog that was expecting his owner to give him a treat. Then he saw, and threw his head back, laughing until he was braying—braying like some kind of deranged donkey.

I looked down at the spot where my hammer had struck. The new spot was just above the old bruise, halfway to the end of the nail. There was a little crack there, ragged and angry-looking. Some of the nail had broken away, and I could see the red flesh underneath, already starting to swell.

Carl got his laughter under control long enough to say, "Didn't anyone tell you? Pound the nail, not the hand!" Then I could see the wheels turning behind his eyes. "Hey, maybe that's why your girl left you. Maybe you just can't pound anything right!"

The thumb went to my mouth, and my tongue found the rough edge where the nail had broken away. The harness strained against my weight, and as I sat back, I could see Quinn standing up and looking in our direction. He looked at me, my thumb in my mouth like a toddler, then over to Carl, his head thrown back, his body straining against his own harness. His cheeks went red.

"That's it, Carl. You're off. Get your gear and get off my roof!"

Carl stopped laughing immediately, but I hurt too much to take any pleasure in it. I sucked on my thumb, seeing stars, while Carl stuttered over an explanation.

"Quinn...I didn't do any—"

"Yeah, I see what you didn't do. Now get your gear and get down before I throw you down!"

Carl looked into the older man's eyes, trying to judge if the threat was real. He must have seen that it was, because he didn't give so much as a sound after that. He just slid his hammer into the loop of his belt, unhooked his harness, and sulked off in the direction of the ladder.

Something warm and wet began to trickle down the edge of my lip. I pulled the thumb away, and it seemed to tug at my tongue like one of those sticker bushes that pulls against your jeans in the springtime. I looked at it again, but there was no blood, only the wet indentation of flesh inside the crack above the bruise.

It was my tongue that was bleeding.

Two days later, that roof was done and we moved on to the next. A new roof meant laying down the plywood decking before we could do anything else. We split into two-man teams, one to hold the piece against the frame while the other measured and cut it down to fit. Quinn picked me to hold, and I was thankful for it. It was an easy job, without much chance of screwing up as long as your arms stayed strong and your hands stayed out of the way. All of it meant less hammering, and I was thankful for that, too.

I wasn't sleeping at night. I could say that it was because of the pain, and that would be enough of the truth for most people. This time the pain didn't go away, and every waking moment I could feel the blood pounding inside the thumb. It was broken, maybe. I couldn't be sure. I had some pills left over from when I had wrenched my back the year before, and I ate them like they were candy. They didn't make a difference. I could still feel the thing throbbing, like something that was alive all on its own.

But it wasn't just the pain that kept me up at night. In fact, the pain was just a sideshow, little more than a distraction from what was going on inside my head. My thoughts had become wild and vicious. It wasn't enough anymore that I was just thinking about killing Anna. Now I was *planning* it. In my mind I could see myself, walking up the stairs to the little apartment above the Laundromat that she was sharing with the latest poor bastard. Over and over again I pried open the door with the claw of my hammer, and the scene felt so real that sometimes I could even hear the snap of the wood as the latch tore free. The two of them were asleep, lying naked, drenched in sweat. It was nothing to bring the hammer down, again and again and again, sometimes with the head, but sometimes with the claw, each time taking pleasure in the wet cracking sounds it made as it struck their bodies.

In those fantasies, they never even had time to move.

Yet through it all, through every one of those deranged imaginings, I could sense that those thoughts were not solely my own. Another voice nagged against the back of my mind, faint, but growing stronger by the day, and when I heard it, I would look down at that smashed thumb, at the cracked-red grin where the nail had split, and the unblinking eye below it.

For in my waking dreams, when I held the hammer that ended Anna's life, it was not in my right hand, but in my left, and every time I raised it, I could see that eye beneath the thumbnail, staring into me. I kept it covered most of the time. That did nothing to quiet the voice, but it helped not having to look at it. At work, my gloves were always on, and when I got home, I wrapped it tight in a heavy cloth bandage. I'd take my pills and turn the TV on as loud as it would go, and try to focus on anything that didn't involve Anna or the thumb. But that was impossible.

Because beneath the bandage, I could feel the thing moving.

All these thoughts seemed to drown away in the whine of the saw. On the roof, that other voice seemed quieter, more distant. I could still hear it, but compared to the sounds of work around me, it was little more than a whisper. The sun was at my back, and I began to feel like a human being again. I closed my eyes, and all the pain and fear—fear of what I might do—began to wash away.

Then I heard the saw stop, and something about the sound worried me. I opened my eyes and when I looked down, all the fear came back to me at once, and stronger than before.

The plywood sheet was only half cut through. At the end of the cut sat the saw, still now, held in the hand of Ben Jackson, whose eyes were wide and staring at me in a mixture of disbelief and fear. In the path of the blade sat my left hand. Somehow, it had moved from its gripping point at the bottom of the sheet, moved while my eyes had been closed. Now it lay, palm flat against the wood, directly in the path of the saw blade. Against the edge of the blade sat the thumb, only an instant away from being severed.

Ben stared at my face, telling me wordlessly his disbelief of what had almost happened—what, if not for his quick reflexes, surely *would have* happened. My other arm was straining to keep the board in place, and yet I could not bring myself to move. I just stared down at my hand, and at the thumb still lying in the path of the blade.

Beneath the glove, I could feel it begin to shift.

———◆———

Carl came back, just like I knew he would. He'd been gone little more than a week since that day Quinn had put him down the ladder, and when he came back up it was fifteen minutes late for the day's work. Quinn saw him come up, but pretended not to, which told me everything I needed to know about the reasons behind his return. I'd expected to hear Carl gloating about how he'd gotten one over on the old man, or at least to be wearing that monkey-fuck grin he never seemed to be without. Instead, he found a spot on the line without a word and hooked his safety line onto the metal ring that had been set there for the purpose. He didn't look at me at all, and he avoided Quinn completely.

He wasn't the only one avoiding the old man. I had taken to staying out of Quinn's line of sight too, but for me it was out of fear for what his sharp old eyes might see. That other voice in my head—the voice of the thumb, because by then I was sure that that was what it was—had gotten stronger. It kept me up at night, and what little sleep I could find was filled with terrible nightmares. They were nightmares of what I might do, what surely I *would* do if that other voice had its way. When I looked in the mirror, I could see how my eyes had sunken inward, how the bones of my cheeks seemed to jut out from lost sleep and lost weight.

Surely, Quinn had seen at least some of it. A blind man could tell I was not quite right, no matter how hard I tried to hide it. It was only a matter of time before Quinn got a good look at my face, at the way I shook with fatigue when I climbed the ladder, and sent me back down once and for all. So I kept out of sight and chose my spot as far away from his as possible. Yet, at the same time, I wanted him to see. I wanted to reach out to him, to call upon his wisdom and his guidance. I needed to tell him, and I needed him to help me.

Because just the night before, I had awakened with blood on my shirt, and my fear was that it wasn't my own.

The whole time, I kept the thumb hidden, hoping that by denying it, I could make those dreams and those thoughts simply go away. But even beneath the bandage, I could feel it moving, and I could hear it plotting. That day with the saw had not been an accident, and I knew now that it wanted to be rid of me as much as I wanted to be rid of it. It whispered to me, told me its plans in a voice that was almost kind, but when I heard it, I only wrapped the bandage tighter.

I sleepwalked through my days, relying on years spent on the slopes and the memory of my muscles to keep me safe. Still, I depended too much on the safety harness, and if not for the strength of that nylon line my problems would have ended a dozen times, spread out on the cracked and stony ground below. Quinn hadn't seen it, but Carl had, and when I caught him looking at me, he would lower his head quickly and get on with his work. But I knew he was only waiting, thinking about how to turn what he knew to his own advantage. He blamed me for the way Quinn had treated him. That much I was sure of. It was only a matter of time before he would try to get even.

But the thumb was throbbing too much for me to give Carl more than passing attention. I could feel the blood pulsing inside it—my blood, growing thick and foul beneath the skin. It shifted inside the glove and I could feel the hard-nail beak of its mouth gnawing. The fabric pulled and stretched as it worked, biting away at the cloth until it began to rip.

Without thinking, I tore the glove off. The nail had gone completely black, except for the red gash of its mouth, and the angry pool of its eye, which fixed itself on me. It stared into me and, though I wanted to, I could not look away. The voice was louder now, telling me about Anna, telling me about Carl, telling me about the two of them together in obscene detail. There was no doubt of the things it knew, and yet there was no way it could know. But the voice was sure, and it was strong, and as it spoke the words I believed them.

Somehow a noise broke through the haze of my thoughts. It was a shuffle of feet, stopping behind me. I didn't have to turn around to know it was Carl. I looked up to see that we were alone on the roof. Quinn must have given the call for lunch, but with the thumb's voice in my head I hadn't heard. I looked down at the shadow I cast across the rooftop, at the shadow of Carl behind me, of his hand coming up above his shoulder, above my head.

I spun, and as I spun, the hammer collided with his side and sent him stumbling. His eyes went wide and his already upraised arms began to flail. Upraised for what? To strike me? There had been nothing in his hand. In that instant before his eyes showed panic, there had been no threat of mischief, but the beginnings of an apology. Had he only come to tell me something, something he could only say to me when no one else was looking?

It didn't matter now, because he was falling. I had caught him off balance, and at the edge of the slope there was nothing for him to grab hold of, no room to plant his feet. One of those feet brushed against the edge and slipped. He seemed to fall backward in slow motion, and as he did, I had time to wonder why he had been so close to the edge in the first place. My God, didn't he know not to sneak up on someone so close to the drop?

I made a grab for him and my fingers found the nylon strap of his safety line that lay unhooked and dangling from his chest. The flat cord dug into my hand as the rest of his body tumbled over the side. Then I felt myself surge forward, and in that instant I thought that I might go right over the edge with him. My own line yanked taut against the added weight, and I felt it start to slide through the buckles that kept it secured to my middle. My right hand shot out and grabbed it, and my shoulders strained between the two lines as if I was a victim on the rack.

I was close to the edge now. Looking down I could see Carl flailing, his arms and legs searching for purchase where there was none. He grabbed onto the line, and in his panic tried to pull himself up. His feet scrabbled against the wall only to slide back down again. He reached up for the overhang of the roof, but he was already too far down.

Then I felt his line begin to slip in my hand. Carl must have felt it too, because he stopped flailing and looked up at me with horror in his eyes. I grabbed the line tighter, and as I looked down at my hand I could see the thumb. Instead of clamping down on the line it was sticking out like a hitchhiker's, and I could not make it move. The nylon slipped again, and my hand and shoulders began to burn with pain. I summoned all my will and every last ounce of strength I had to clamp the thumb down, because without it I could not hold onto the line much longer. But it would not move, and as I looked at it I could see the corners of its foul, red mouth curl into a grin.

Carl looked up at me again, this time with a new look in his eyes. What I saw there was a silent plea, a begging of forgiveness for everything that had gone between us before. It was a promise that he would never be unkind again if I would only help him now. I wanted to help him, and I clenched with all the strength in the four fingers that were still mine. But it was not enough.

The line slid from my grip, slashing against my palm like a knife. The pleading look in Carl's eyes stayed locked on me as he fell, three stories, to the ground. When his body hit, I heard the crunch of bone, saw the impossible angles that his legs and neck made, and I knew that he was dead. My palm was bleeding, and my fingers closed in reflex around the wound. But the thumb was already there, tucked inside like a sleeping animal.

As I watched the others begin to gather around Carl's body, I could hear the thumb as it started to drink.

Quinn called me twice in the weeks after. He told me I should come back to work, that there was still a spot for me on the line and I could have it any time I was ready. He said that it wasn't my fault, and that no one blamed me for what happened. He said these things into my answering machine, because I would not answer the phone. I sat in my chair and watched the tape spin, and I knew that I would never call him back.

He said that it was just an accident, but I knew better.

I don't leave the house much anymore. Mostly I just sit in my chair and try not to listen to the things that the thumb tells me. It talks to me all the time now. It tells me things I'm glad no one else can hear. I try not to listen, and I try not to fall asleep, either. The last time I did, I woke up in the kitchen with my hand reaching for the drawer where I keep the long butcher knife. I thought, not for the first time, about using that knife to be rid of the thumb once and for all. Then I heard the thing whispering in my thoughts and knew that I could not.

After all, that's exactly what it wants me to do.

So I sit, and I tighten down the bandages until the circulation stops and the whole hand goes numb. That's usually enough to quiet the voice long enough for me to think, if only for a few moments. And for those times when it's not enough, well, that's what the hammer is for. It never strays from my right hand, and when I raise it, that's when the whispering stops. Because there's one thing I've proven time and again, one thing that the thumb knows without a doubt.

I know exactly how to use it.

Swallow

I SHOULD HAVE KEPT my mouth shut, impossible as it may have been. I was in love with the sound of my own voice then, so convinced of my own intellectual superiority that I was forever correcting people's pronunciations and running roughshod over opinions that differed even slightly from my own. Had I been capable of even the smallest amount of restraint, just one step beyond the borders of my own ego, I might have prevented all that came after. As it happened, I can only remember my words, and be filled with shame.

"It makes sense if you'd just think about it," I said. Van and Goldman were grinning by then, catching on to the fun I was having at the expense of old Warren. Poor Warren, who sat there, holding the napkin to the corner of his mouth, hanging on my every word. Warren, who was both subject and eager audience of the joke I was about to make.

"The mouth is a sensitive organ." Here Van let out a cough to cover a laugh, no doubt at the use of *mouth* and *organ* in the same sentence. "It's more complex than people give it credit for. It has to talk and chew and taste; not easy stuff, any of it. The amount of brain power it takes for just one of those things has to be staggering, and to do all at once, it's as good as saying it has a mind all its own."

Warren's own mouth was open now, heedless of the blood that had started to trickle out of it and onto his chin. Goldman shot me a look that asked if I was going to say something about it, but his intimate knowledge of my character should have told him I wouldn't. The joke would be so much more complete, so much more satisfying, if I just left it alone. Besides, I had my rhythm now, and the line on which I hauled in my victim was slackening.

"And the tongue! Think about it! Day in and day out, from the moment you're born until the moment you die, it just lays there. You put food in your mouth and you taste it, but what happens the rest of the time? It's not as if you have an off switch that stops it from doing what it does."

"Tho?" Warren had found the trickle and pressed the hand-kerchief to his mouth as he spoke. The boys were doing all they could to keep it in, but my own face was a practiced mask of sincerity.

"So," I continued, "you've got food in your mouth, what? Five percent of the time. Maybe ten if you're Van."

"Hey!" Van took his cue and played the line with near-perfect indignation.

"So, what is it tasting the other ninety-five percent of the time? Itself. The inside of your mouth. Your lips. Your teeth. The insides of your cheeks. It's tasting them all the time, only, your brain blocks it all out, because if you had to taste all of that, every hour of every day, it would drive you mad."

Sparks began to fire behind his eyes as the beginnings of uneasy understanding tugged at his slack features. There was a question there, and with the other two silently egging me on, I was all too happy to supply the answer.

"But there still has to be some part of you that *does* taste it, some part buried safely at the back of your subconscious where the rest of your mind can't find it. Maybe after all these years, that part of you is finally starting to come forward and assert itself."

Here I paused, savoring the look that had gone from uneasiness to horror, watching my friends, those two perfect cronies, as they vibrated on the edge of hilarity just over his shoulder. I looked at each of them in turn, feeling my triumph as I delivered my final line.

"Maybe that's why you keep biting the inside of your lip. Maybe you like the way you taste."

Warren pulled the handkerchief away from his mouth and looked down at the reddish brown spot that had soaked its way into the weave. The dull look on his face was all the justification I needed for taking advantage of him. By all the rules of the world that I and my schoolmates knew, he should have had everything. He had even been named for greatness: Warren Wollcott the Third, pegged at birth to be the shining light of a family that already glowed with its own brightness. Only, he couldn't live up to the expectations the name carried with it, and no amount of money paid in favors and endowments to headmasters by Warren Wollcott the Second would ever transform him into anything more than what he was: a trust fund boob who couldn't so much as chew a piece of bread without biting the inside of his mouth.

Small wonder then, that Van, Goldman and I locked onto him. One might even say that it was Warren who brought the three of us together. Despite the differences in our situations and backgrounds, we were united in our need to find someone who was lesser than us, at least in our own eyes. For our various reasons, each known only to ourselves, we needed someone to keep close, someone who, by comparison, would make us feel like so much more than what we were.

Warren fit that bill in spades. From that very first day more than a year past, he gave no sign that he recognized our attentions as anything other than friendship. So naïve, so trusting was he in his outlook, that he began to seek us out long after we had grown bored with him. He was never far from our sides, his trundling steps a sharp counterpoint to the forced casualness of our own. He took our increasingly vicious swipes at him, always unaware, always hanging on our every word.

But this time was different somehow. There should have been a smile, a sign that his awareness was slowly catching up to our own. There should have been a look, free of anger or embarrassment, that would absolve us of the wrong we had committed. Instead, there was only that blank stare, and a sense that something profound was happening behind those eyes.

There was understanding in that stare, and something that looked like terror, as if something had dawned on him, some universal truth that had been hidden, a change to his worldview that he was not ready to face. Van and Goldman looked on, their own smiles slackening, silent questions in their eyes asking how the joke had gone so far so suddenly. We watched him walk away from us, that trundling step more halting, uncertain, and knew somehow, all of us, that things would not be the same again.

———◆———

We didn't see much of Warren after that. We waited on campus in the usual spots, expecting to see his familiar form round the corner at any moment, always disappointed when the moment never came. Soon it became clear that Warren was avoiding us, and though none of us could know what it was about my joke that had evoked such a strong reaction in our mascot, we knew that, until we could reach him, until some apology could be given and some penance paid, our comfortable situation would never again be what it had been.

Goldman used his considerable charms to pry Warren's class schedule from a homely administrative aide. Van, the natural sycophant, spoke to his teachers. I made enquiries among his classmates. If anyone had noticed him in the first place, they had no idea where he'd hidden himself now. The fall stretched on with no sign of him, and as the leaves fell from the trees, we began to fear the worst. None of us spoke of it openly, but they wore their accusations clearly when they thought I wasn't looking. It was my fault that he was gone. Whatever had happened to him, whatever would happen to him, I alone was the cause.

It was Christmas break before Warren finally emerged from hiding. Van had returned to his family on one coast while Goldman used his own vacation to good advantage on the other. My own circumstances were such that I was left to my own devices on campus, and as a matter of course spent my days alone in the library, reading random passages from dead writers in a corner I had staked out for the purpose. There, tucked away in my little ersatz den, is where he found me.

At first, I was almost at a loss to recognize him. Gone was the bounce, the eagerness in his step. He walked quickly and deliberately, his chin tucked tight against his chest, his hands thrust deep into the pockets of his tattered overcoat. When he finally looked up at me, it was with eyes that had sunken into his face. How much weight he had lost, I couldn't tell. Twenty pounds? Thirty pounds? The overcoat hid all but the hollowed-out cheeks and the bony sockets of his eyes.

Still, the sight of him made me bolt up out of my seat. I wanted to run to him, to embrace him. Only in that moment did I know how much I had depended on him, on his mere presence. Without him, without Van and Goldman to focus my attention, I was aimless. I wanted to reach out, to touch him just to be sure that he was real. As it was, I could only manage to say his name. "Warren."

"It's not true," he said.

His voice was little more than a whisper, as if the energy, the very life behind it had been drained away. Drugs were my first thought. Drugs or some chronic illness. Little else could explain the transformation he had gone through in the three intervening months.

"What's not true?"

"What you said. What you told me. It can't be right." For an instant I thought he was going to hit me, such was his posture and the determined set of his jaw. But his arms stayed locked as his sides, his hands buried deep in his coat pockets.

"Warren, what are you talking about?"

"You know!" Only I didn't know. I couldn't know. The details of our prior associations, the specifics of my crimes against him, had completely faded from memory. Only the fact of Warren's absence remained, and now that he was back I could barely think what to say. Yet, the insistence, the sheer desperation of his words told me that I ought to know, that some critical truth was within my grasp, if only I could remember what it was.

"You have to," he went on. "You have to know, because, if it's true... It can't be true! So, if it's not true, you can tell me and it will just be one of those things, and we can laugh about it and everything's going to be okay. But you have to help me. You have to tell me how to stop it!"

I know now what I should have said. I should have told him that it wasn't true, no matter that I didn't know what it was I'd be denying. None of it was true. The world was not true. The ground, the earth, the very air, all of it not true if that was what he needed to hear me say. But I didn't say it, and I couldn't say it. My need for precision, for unassailable correctness, overrode whatever small sense of compassion or conscience I had.

"Warren," I told him, "I don't know what you're talking about."

His eyes went wide, and the look in them told me that my betrayal could not have been more complete had I stabbed him in his very heart. He froze there, staring, and again I cannot help but believe that in that moment I had yet another chance to save him if only I had recognized it. But I didn't, and when the moment was gone, he turned from me, moaning something low and pained through clenched teeth. I caught him by the elbow as he turned, and his arm slid from its pocket.

He pulled away from me with a strength betrayed by his hunched frame and narrowed features. His free arm trailed behind him like the tail of a kite as he ran, and at its end I could see his fingers, ragged and torn. The nails were bitten bloody, and his wrist was covered in scratches.

New Year's Day came and went, and students returned in a slow trickle that at once became a flood. Goldman and Van came back from their respective pursuits, and the three of us gave one last try at our old ways. We knew it was futile, doomed despite all our wishing otherwise. I didn't tell them about my encounter with Warren. Telling them would have compounded my shame, but worse, it would have given us all false hope. In our hearts, we all knew that we could never return to what once was.

Winter melted into spring, and I melted with it into the shadows and corners of the campus. I stopped going out at night, stopped speaking in class. What few women approached me, I shrugged away. The penance was no less than I deserved, a fact underscored by the phone calls I received at odd times, always in the middle of the night. In the long silence before the hangup, I sometimes thought that I heard sobbing at the other end of the line.

As summer approached, it brought with it all the excitement of impending freedom. To everyone, that was, except me. I knew I wouldn't be free, could never be free, until I spoke with Warren again. It had taken me most of the spring to half-convince myself that whatever had afflicted him over break had passed now, that those silent phone calls were motivated by embarrassment rather than need. I resolved to go to him, and when the next call came, I made note of the number.

I tracked it back to a small, one bedroom house at the edge of campus. No doubt it had been purchased by Warren's father for far more than it was worth simply because of its proximity to the school. To know that he had been this close the whole time only compounded my shame, and gave volume to the voice inside me that said I should not have waited so long.

The front yard was newly-mown, its edges immaculate. The sight gave a brief lift to my spirits until I realized that its keepers were likely hired men the Wollcotts kept on retainer. They did their work unbidden so long as the checks kept coming, oblivious to anything that might be going on inside. On the stoop were bundles of unclaimed mail held together with rubber bands. Somehow I knew that knocking on the door would bring no answer. I tried the knob, and the door swung back into darkness.

I was five steps in before the smell hit me. It was a thick, cloying smell, like old meat mixed with human waste. Something pungent came with it that stung my eyes. If I had been able to eat anything in the preceding days, I surely would have parted with it then. As it was, I managed to retch up no more than a thin line of spittle, which I wiped away with my sleeve.

As my eyes adjusted to the darkness, I searched for the source of the smell. The drapes in the front room had been closed against the sunlight, but apart from that one detail, there was nothing about the look of the place to suggest anything so foul. It was immaculate, like a parlor in a funeral home, like a museum display, set in place and then left alone, not meant to be touched by human hands.

I moved farther inside, and as I did, the smell grew stronger. I felt the tingle in my legs as the blood rushed into them, readying me to flee. It was coming from the kitchen. I was sure of it now. All of my senses screamed at me to run, but my guilt goaded me on, telling me that whatever I would find there was of my own making.

There was more light beyond the kitchen door. It streamed in between the slats of the blinds and bathed the place in a pale gold glow. As I pushed the door aside, I was met with the low droning of flies. Smears of something, now dried black, streaked the floors. They marked a trail between the refrigerator and sink, counting the passage of time with layer upon layer, stain upon stain. More smudges of the same stuff dotted the counters and the fridge door. I took them for handprints, but something about the assessment hit me wrong. The thought vanished as soon as it came, for my eyes had found the corner of the room where the trail ended. There, beneath the phone that hung from the wall, a lone figure huddled, shivering.

I took a tentative step inside. If the thing on the floor knew I was there, it gave no indication. It was drawn into itself to the point where I could not guess its shape, and its breath came in ragged gasps weighed down by heavy sobs. Another step, and I suddenly realized what it was about those handprints that seemed so wrong: so many of them had the wrong number of fingers.

"Warren?"

The figure started, and as it did, a cloud of flies stirred from a pile of something thick and clotted nearby. The sound of them made my stomach churn again, and once more I felt my legs ready themselves to run.

The thing on the floor uncurled from its fetal position, propping itself up with first one arm, then the other. It was naked, its skin streaked with dried blood and feces. The hair on its head was long and patchy, as if large chunks had been torn out by the roots. With movements slow and marked by pain, it tuned to face me.

Its cheekbones jutted beneath the dry stretch of its skin. Below them, teeth flashed in the dim light. Where there should have been lips to keep them hidden, there was only ragged flesh, bitten and torn high against the gums. More teeth worked behind a tattered hole where its cheek should have been. With nothing to hold them back, those teeth seemed to grin at me.

Still, in its eyes I could see something of the human being it still was. Those eyes pleaded with me, the desperation in them a sharp contrast to the ever-smiling mouth below. The eyes told me the very thing which I had feared from the moment

I had seen its shape on the floor. They told me that this was my friend. They told me that he had been expecting me.

"Warren."

His eyes widened, and in them I could see something of joy, something of relief. His chest shuddered and the air escaping from his throat sounded like something between a laugh and a sigh. He held out his hands to me. They were fingerless hands whose bloody stumps had been bitten ragged over and over again, and between them there was a knife.

I started at the sight of it, and had enough of my faculties left to ask myself why, of all things in that room, the knife should be the one to cause such a reaction. Warren saw my fright, and began to shake his head. He moaned, a low sound, wet and guttural, and somehow I knew that he had no tongue left with which to form the words. He held his hands out to me, his palms pressed together as if in prayer, the knife between them, blade down, its handle offered to me.

At once I saw the pleading in his eyes, the questioning tilt of his head. He looked down to his lap, and I followed his gaze past the ladders of his ribs, the distended hump of his stomach. I looked at the series of little cuts he had made there, and only then understood how he intended me to use the knife.

He looked at me once more, and I could see the hunger there, the desperate eyes above flashing teeth. His arms were still held out to me, and along them I could see the bite marks, the flesh that had been torn and laid open to the bone, every part his teeth could reach gnawed and ragged. Yet, there was a happiness, too, in those eyes, a sense that I of all people could help him, that I alone *would* help him.

He gave me the knife because I could get to all the places he could not.

A moment passed, our two forms frozen in the golden half-light. Warren's hope gave way to confusion, and finally to panic. As the knife fell and clattered on the floor, there were tears in his eyes. He fell forward, cupped his face in what was left of his hands, and heaved with wordless sobs.

———◇———

Thirty minutes later, I saw my last of Warren. The paramedics loaded him into the back of the ambulance after pumping him full of sedatives and heaving their stomachs dry onto the kitchen floor. Beneath the plastic oxygen mask, those teeth still grinned, and those eyes looked back at me, accusing. The paramedics had questions. The police had questions. I told them I didn't know.

I sat on Warren's porch and watched the cars and their lights as they sped away out of sight. He would find a way to kill himself. Of that much I was certain, as certain as I was that the blame of it lay squarely on my head. I had brought him to this place, but in the end I could not give him what he asked of me. Maybe that was the worst betrayal of all.

I closed my eyes and squeezed them shut, hoping that if I could squeeze them hard enough, I could drive away the sight of those teeth, those eyes. When I finally opened them, the cars and their lights were gone, and I was alone on the empty street. I sat there a long time before I noticed that my jaw was clenched tight, and I could taste my own tongue as it started to bleed.

Ten and Gone

TWO HITS WITH THE bump key and the door popped open like it had never been locked. It was a cheap Connor entry set, the kind that contractors bought in bulk. It was a best-case scenario, better than Marcus had dared to hope for. He straightened, adopting the air that he had every right to be there, on this stranger's porch in the middle of the night, lockpick in hand and a flashlight on his belt. He listened for the beeping of an alarm that he knew would never come. They always installed the alarms later, if they installed them at all, and this place was new, so new that he could smell the fresh paint as he stepped in over the threshold.

10

The subdivision had come up quick, a tidy little enclave of McMansions built to sell for two-and-a-half, maybe three million each. Marcus had been watching the site for weeks and even prowled around it a time or two after dark, hunting for stray power tools. Most of them were half-finished with bare studs and plastic undersiding still showing, but not this one.

No, with this one he'd hit the jackpot. The place was finished all the way down to the custom brass light switches and lit up like a Christmas tree with all the new owners' possessions stacked in neatly labeled boxes.

It would be a quick score, maybe even a good score if he was lucky enough to find a safe that hadn't been bolted to the floor or a jewelry box tucked away in the corner of the master bedroom. He needed a good score now, maybe more than he ever had. A beefy custom stereo or a box of Louboutin shoes. If it was here, he'd find it, and he'd find it fast. Ten minutes was all he'd ever needed in a house. His internal clock was as good as a stopwatch. Ten minutes to grab the best stuff and get out. Ten minutes and he'd be gone.

He crossed the foyer and took the steps of the central staircase two at a time, paying no mind to the way his heavy footsteps rang against the rough tile and crunched on the carpeting. Most of the best stuff was sure to be on the first floor, but if there was something that the new owners held especially dear, they would have moved it upstairs before anything else. He'd passed a few boxes in the foyer marked "baby toys" in big, cartoon bubble-letters, and made a mental note to check them on the way out for anything that he might be able to bring back to Trina as a peace offering. Maybe a teddy bear or one of those little stuffed dogs with the big heads and the sad eyes that she used to collect back in high school. If he came back with one of those for the baby, she might leave the chain off the door when she talked to him. She might even let him back inside to share the bed again.

He paused at the top of the stairs to get his bearings. Wide landing. Short hallway to either side. Master suite on one end. Two, maybe three bedrooms on the other. He'd take the big room first and sweep through the others on his way back. There were paintings on the walls, and he took a few seconds to eyeball each one. He didn't know art, but could usually make a fair guess and pick one that would sell. None of these were it though, just blurry figures rendered in clumsy brushstrokes, like out-of-focus photographs. Amateur work set in ornate frames to make them look valuable. The wife was a painter, he guessed, which meant they could afford for her to be a painter. It boded well for his chances of finding jewelry in the bedroom. He might even be able to offload a few of the frames once he'd ditched the paintings inside. One of them was already empty, just hanging crooked in the center of the landing like a wide-open window.

9

He strode toward the master suite, wondering, not for the first time, what kind of job someone had to have to afford a place like this one, with its high ceilings and its light fixtures that looked like they'd come straight out of a palace. Something a damn sight better than anything he'd ever been able to hold down, and probably a lot cushier, too. The problem with guys who had jobs like that, and places like this, was that they never appreciated them. He'd bet this whole take that the guy was on some shrink's couch every week whining about how rough he had it, never knowing that someone like Marcus was out there, just waiting for the right time to bump his lock open and take everything that wasn't nailed down. With any luck the guy would have plenty to talk about at his next appointment.

The door to the bedroom was open, but he paused there out of habit, listening for anyone who might be inside, calculating the time it would take to get back down the stairs if he heard a voice. But there was no one here. He'd watched the place for hours, sitting up the road in his white van, looking for warning signs and finding none. The only odd thing had been the light, shining out of every window, almost too bright. No doubt they'd wanted to make it look like someone was home, but without a car in the driveway or any motion inside at all, it might as well have been a beacon.

The bedroom was big, too big for Marcus' taste, with an ornate, king-sized bed and carpet so plush that his feet sank into it as he walked. Who needed this much space just to sleep? It was almost enough to make him mad, especially when he thought about Trina and the baby in that ratty little one-bedroom apartment. But that was okay. Being mad quieted down that nagging little voice that told him he ought to feel guilty for being here. Being mad made it easier.

The bed was made, and it struck him as odd how finished it seemed, but not so odd that he let it slow him down. It was the closet he was after, and it did not disappoint. It was big enough to be a bedroom all on its own and lined with his stuff on one side and hers on the other two. Nice shoes. *Expensive* shoes. A few of the Loubatins he'd been after. Manolos and Jimmy Choos, too. Enough to make this trip worthwhile all by themselves. He yanked the cover off the bed and piled them all in the center of it, trying not to smile too much, trying not to get ahead of himself when there was still so much left to be done.

8

He'd been hoping for jewelry, or maybe a laptop or two, but no such luck. He had the shoes bundled in the sheet, which he slung over his shoulder like a bargain basement Santa Claus as he bounded down the stairs, but that was all. Not even the clothes had been worth taking. They looked expensive, but were cheap to the touch and slippery like cut-rate vinyl. It didn't matter. He still had the rest of the house, and now that he had the lay of the place he was starting to map out his route in his head. Upstairs again first. Two, three minutes, tops. Then a quick sweep through the dining room to find the box that held the silver and China plates. Grab the TV from the living room and anything else worth having along the way.

He dropped the shoes in the foyer, where he'd decided to make a staging area, and started back up the stairs. His initial shot of adrenaline was starting to wear off. If something was going to go wrong, it would have happened by now. But he was in the clear with almost eight minutes left and didn't have to rush. Still, he took the steps two at a time. He must have stepped in something sticky along the way, because he could feel the way his boots clung to the carpet as he went. Insurance would pay for the carpet, he knew. Insurance would pay for all of it, the lucky bastards. He'd never had insurance, never had anything worth insuring. Not until now, anyway. Maybe he'd get enough from this score to make this time the last time. Maybe—

He froze two steps from the top. His adrenaline surged. There was a box on the landing. It hadn't been there before. He was sure of it. It was right in the middle of his path and he would have remembered having to step over it. There was no way he could have missed it, either on the way up or on the way back down. And yet, there it was, a squat little cube of cardboard with the flaps hanging loose. Scrawled across its front in unsteady black letters were the words GOOD STUFF.

7

He stood statue-still, listening to the quiet as the clock ticked down in his head. Someone had put the box there, which meant that there was someone here, inside the house with him. And yet, he heard nothing but the sound of his own breath and the thudding of his pulse in his ears. If someone was here, he should have been able to feel it, the same way that you could feel when someone was trying to sneak up behind you in a quiet room. But there was no one. The doors had not moved and everything down to the paintings on the walls was exactly as he had left it. Everything except for this new box, this box of GOOD STUFF.

He crept his way up the last two steps, breathing shallow and quiet, wincing at the sticky sound of his boots as they pulled at the carpet. Something glinted beneath the loose flaps of the box, and he crouched low to get a closer look. If this was a trap, this was when it would spring. A woman with a baseball bat over her shoulder. A policeman with his pistol drawn. But there was nothing in the stillness but empty air. He reached out and the flaps fell aside, limp and heavy, like wet leaves.

He let out a low whistle, forgetting all caution as he got a look at what was inside. Here was the jewelry he had been hoping for, great tangles of it, heaped together like a jumble of old electrical cords. Gold chains caught the light from the chandelier as he turned them over in his hands. Diamonds and sapphires gleamed along their lengths like drops of morning dew. He scooped it up like water from a river, and there was more of it than he could hold with both hands.

It couldn't be real. There was too much of it, and it was too haphazardly jumbled in the box to be anything but cheap, costume stuff. And yet, the weight of it was right, and the stones were bright and clear. He wasn't an expert, but he knew glass gems when he saw them. These were not glass gems, and even the stingiest fence, at pennies on the dollar, would trade them for more money than he had ever seen in his life. It would be enough money to get him and Trina out of that crappy apartment, enough to get the baby a room of her own with flowers on the walls and a crib full of toys and a mobile strung with tiny bears to watch over her while she slept.

6

He gathered up the box. It was warm to the touch and it came up from the carpet with the same sticky tearing sound that his boots had made on the stairs. All by itself, the box made this a better job than any he had done before, and though six minutes were left on his internal clock there was no need for him to stick around any longer. He bounded back down to the foyer. With each step he cradled the box closer and cared less where it had come from. It could have been on the landing the whole time. In his haste he might have stepped right past it. It was odd, true, but he had seen enough odd things in this business to know that odd things happened every day. But this was it. He was done, and maybe for good. He'd bundle the box and the shoes into the van and drive away. He'd drive away and never come back, not to this place, not to any other place he had to break his way into. He'd go back to Trina and find a way to make her listen, to tell her all the things he'd never been able to find words for. She'd take him back and he'd be done, once and for all.

He paused at the bottom of the stairs as he sensed a change in the air, a shift in pressure like a door being opened in a distant room. With it came a familiar sound, a high, hitching wail that drifted down from the second story hallway.

It was the sound of a baby crying.

He froze, the box heavy in his arms, as he waited for the soft pad of footsteps on the carpet, for the answering words of a mother, perhaps a father. If he was lucky, those footsteps would come from the second floor, and he'd have time to reach his van with the box still in his hands, time to be away from this place before they even knew he was here. If he was unlucky, the footsteps would come from this floor, from just around the corner. And what would he do then? Would he fight? Would he take the box and try to run? Now that he had it, he couldn't imagine letting go of the little box and the jumble of treasure inside. He would fight for it. He would have to fight, or he would lose everything.

But the footsteps never came. He held his breath and watched through the entryways for shadows on the far walls, but there was no one there. There was only the child, the sound of its cries rising and falling, only to rise again more urgently, over and over again.

5

He made up his mind then to go. All he needed was the box. He could leave the shoes behind. He could leave the whole place behind, with its odd paintings and the strange smell in the air. But his feet would not move. The baby was still crying and no one was coming for it. At once he thought that the child had been left there on purpose, but the thought seemed absurd. No one moved into a brand new house only to abandon a baby. But then, no one jumbled a fortune's worth of jewelry into a cardboard box and labeled it GOOD STUFF. All the rules he was used to didn't seem to apply to this place. The baby cried and no one came for it, even though someone had to be there, had to have set this box in his way. The baby cried, and with each breath it sounded more and more like the baby that he and Trina had made.

Before he could stop himself he was climbing up the stairs. His steps felt heavy, the soles of his boots so sticky that he thought he might bring the carpet up with him as he moved. The baby's wailing grew louder as he drew near. He was convinced now that it was a little girl, no more than a few weeks old. In his mind he could see her with her fists balled, her face scrunched and red. He crept across the landing toward the sound, past the strange and blurry paintings. They seemed less blurry now, and in one of them he could see familiar outlines, two people posing for their portrait. He'd thought that one of those frames had been empty, but he must have been mistaken.

The door to the bedroom was ajar. He could hear the child's frantic howling just beyond it, growing louder and more urgent by the second. He pushed the door aside by inches, moving slow as if he was wading through water. The door was warm to the touch and it swung aside without a sound.

The shades were drawn and the room was dark, but still he could make out the wooden crib that stood at its center. The room was empty but for that crib, and it struck him then that, out of all the rooms in the house, this was the only one where the lights had been left off. He stepped inside, his boots still sticking to the carpet, his eyes adjusting to the dark. There were flowers painted on the walls, and above the crib a circle of little teddy bears dangled from a mobile like hanged men, turning lazily, casting long shadows.

4

The cries became louder then, so loud that they felt like a dagger driving its way into his brain. He pressed his hands to the sides of his head to keep them at bay. Again he fought the urge to run, and might have given in to it if not for the dark shape that moved just beyond the bars of the crib. In his mind he was sure that it would look just like the baby that Trina had once held out to him, the one she had told him was his. He had run away then, but he would not run away now.

His shadow fell across the bars as he stepped toward the crib. The child inside it shifted and rolled with every hitching breath, with every rising cry. He could see it in the shadows cast by the hanging bears, tiny fists silhouetted against the mattress, tiny legs pumping in rage. He stepped closer, close enough to touch the squirming thing, close enough to gather it into his arms, and yet, for the shadows, he could not see its face.

He reached for the little flashlight on his belt, his mind screaming in tandem with the baby, warning him that he should not be there, that his time was running out, that he should run from this place and not look back. Still, he had to look. He had to know whether this baby was his. He had to look into its tear-filled eyes, to see if there was anything in them of his own.

The flashlight clicked on. He turned its beam on the naked, squirming thing that twitched and writhed in the crib. Where its skin should have been red with anger, it was pale and slick, like an earthworm out in a rainstorm. Stubby fingers clenched and splayed as it moved, and Marcus could see the translucent web of skin that stretched between them. Where he had expected teary eyes, there were no eyes, no face at all. There was only a mouth, stretched into a boneless circle that gaped and yawned with the sounds of its cries.

He stepped back, stumbling, and the thing rose to follow him, dangling at the end of a long stalk that seemed to stretch out from the mattress of the crib like the lure from some deep-sea angler fish. Its limbs fell limp at its sides, a puppet with its strings cut. He could still hear its crying, but the crying was all around him now, everywhere and nowhere at once. Its lips, if they had ever been lips, pulled taut. In the depths behind them were row upon row of hooked and gleaming teeth.

It lashed out at him, the stalk whipping toward his head like a coiled snake. He scrambled back and fell beneath it. As it passed he could smell Trina's perfume on the wind it made, perfume and the scent of the clove cigarettes she would smoke in high school, as if they had been pulled right out of his memories.

3

The thing drew back and Marcus scrambled to his feet, hands and boots sticking to the floor. Or was it the floor that was sticking to him? The doorway to the room was closing, not swinging shut, but puckering, growing smaller by inches. He lunged for it, but fell short as something took hold of his leg and wrenched him backward. He looked back to see the fleshy stalk pulled tight, reeling him back toward the crib. The mouth of the baby-thing had clamped onto to the toe of his boot, and worried at it like a dog gnawing at a bone. The infant body had shrunk to little more than a vague shape, vestigial limbs waving as it tugged and pulled.

He kicked out, and his boot slid down the pulsing length of the stalk like it was slipping through mud. The infant wail still rang in his ears, rising and falling like a siren. He kicked again and found the spot where the baby's eyes should have been. The mouth went slack as the stalk reared back, its plucked-chicken skin gleaming slick in the beam of his dropped flashlight.

Scrambling, he lurched toward the opening. The doorway had been reduced to a tightening circle that grew smaller by the instant. The thing struck out at him once more but he stumbled out of its reach, pulling himself on all fours toward the light of the hallway. He laid a hand on the opening, and it grew teeth beneath his fingers. The infant's cry had become a scream, a high keen of rage and loss that pierced his brain and drove away all rational thought. He heaved himself out into the light, and as his feet slipped through, the teeth snapped together behind him with a hollow crunch.

Chest heaving, he lay on the floor, unable to move, barely able to breathe. The inhuman screaming had stopped, but the echo of it still rang in his ears, in the pulse that played out a painful beat through his skull. He tried to sit up, but the carpet held him down. Muscles trembling, he managed to pull himself away, tiny barbs clinging to his skin like flypaper to a fly. Around him, the walls were peeling back, melting toward the floor like taffy left out in the sun.

2

He staggered to his feet, stumbling out of the hallway and onto the landing, pulling himself along the railing as he moved. It stuck to his hands, and as his palms came away they left little beads of blood behind on the painted wood. The portraits were sliding down the walls, but he could see faces in them now. One of those faces was Trina's, and in the painting she held a bundled infant in her arms. A man stood in the shadows behind her with his hands on her shoulders, but Marcus could not tell if it was meant to be him.

The floor tilted and heaved as he stumbled toward the stairs. The walls flowed down around him. Behind them he could see the new-cut wood of the house's frame, unfinished and skeletal. The only part of this place that's real, he thought. The only part of it that was made with human hands. Whatever the rest of it was, it would swallow him whole if he wasn't quick enough.

Something tugged at his foot as he reached the top of the stairs and he half-slid, half-fell to the foyer below. The chandelier and the other lights had retreated into the skin of the thing, coalescing into bluish orbs that pulsed hypnotically in the darkening space. He closed his eyes for fear that he might lose himself in them. He thought of Trina then, and of the baby, the real baby that he should never have doubted was his own. It gave him the strength to pull himself to his feet. The door, if it had ever been a door at all, was shut tight, but as the walls oozed and shifted around him they made an opening. Beyond it was the night air and the white van that would drive him away from this place. He stepped toward it and felt his ankle give beneath his weight. He winced, but he did not stop.

The letters on the box of GOOD STUFF were just a smear of black now. It rolled on the floor, searching and gnashing, its flaps lined with rows of teeth like curved needles. As the jewelry fell from its mouth it lost its color and fell to ash. He gave no thought to the loss. There was only the opening, the way by which he could finally escape. He lurched toward it, hoping against hope that he still had time.

The opening seemed to sense his approach. Its edges folded together, closing like the mouth of some carnivorous plant. He thrust his hands against its fleshy edges. The house was dark now but for the pulsing blue light, and warm, so warm that he could imagine himself surrendering to it, just letting go and letting the place take him. Still, he fought. His muscles strained until he thought they might snap. He forced the opening wider, wide enough for his head, his shoulders. At last he pushed through. He landed on hard gravel where the concrete porch had been. The skin of the house retreated from its wooden bones as he scrambled away. It collapsed into a sphere that floated in the air, rolling and pulsing like a wet blister in the darkness. It pulsed once more and it was gone, folding in on itself, shrinking down to a single point of light before it disappeared into nothingness.

1

Marcus staggered to his feet, little hitches of unbidden laughter punctuating every breath. His ankle was broken. It wouldn't take his weight as he limped and hopped his way to the white van. He laughed again, high on adrenaline, high on the thought that that thing, whatever it had been, had almost made a meal of him. The idea made him hungry somehow, and he choked back a giggle as he pulled open the driver's door.

He needed a hospital, but the hospital could wait. No, he had to see Trina. Trina and their baby. He wanted to hold her and gather them both into his arms. He found his keys. The ringing in his ears was fading, the wailing of that phantom child gone. There was only the still of the night air, his breathing calm now, controlled. In that moment all his indecision fell away, and his thoughts coalesced into a moment of perfect clarity. He would leave this place, this life, and build a new one with Trina and the baby. He would leave it and he would never look back.

Notice

THERE ARE BETTER WAYS to do this, I know. More acceptable ways. More professional ways. It's strange that, after everything, being seen as professional would be the first thought that comes to my mind as I type this. It's almost funny. When I'm done, you might even think it's funny that the thought occurred to me at all. I'd laugh if I could, but I fear that I've forgotten how.

This will have to serve. As of end of day today, which, if I've planned this correctly, will be just a few minutes before I hit send on this email, I am resigning my position at Essex Interactive. I doubt it will come as a surprise to you or to anyone who's worked with me these past months. Ever since we moved into this new space it's been harder and harder for me to focus on my work. I've made no secret of it, and even if I tried, I'm terrible at hiding such things. I wear my doubts and my fears plain on my face, the way a sad clown wears grease paint. But today, all that has been wiped away, and I'm seeing things clearly for the first time since I can't remember when.

I wanted to give you two weeks' notice. I hope you'll believe me on that point. But time is short, and I can't risk changing my mind.

You've known about my difficulties for a while now. I know you have. The first time I came to you about the low, incessant rumbling coming from Ryan's cubicle, I could tell that you had no idea how to help me. And I'll be the first to admit that I brought an entire suitcase full of emotional baggage to my job that I just wasn't able to leave outside the door. I know that you've had to navigate my anxieties and the ups and downs of my depressive episodes, and through it all you've been patient and kind. Perhaps, had I had anyone else for a boss I might have taken my leave a long time ago.

But I don't blame you. If I can be 100% clear on any point, let it be that one. I don't want to leave you thinking that there's something you might have done differently. All roads were leading to this place, ever since we moved into this building eight months ago.

I couldn't have known it then. Not really. On paper, this old garment factory seemed like the answer to all our prayers. High ceilings. Room to grow. A wide-open loft space that would put any of the other tech companies to shame, and right in the heart of the old district with its old brickwork everywhere and a hipster coffee shop on every corner. Cheap, too. People didn't think I paid much attention to such things, but I talk to the accountants, or at least, I used to. All of them said we were getting it for a steal, even with the renovations and the brand-new heating system.

It's a wonder that that never gave anyone pause.

Because old buildings have a kind of memory, don't they? They stand silent and watch as time marches on around them, and all that time they live and they breathe and they remember it all and not even fire can touch that memory because it sinks down deep into the very bricks. You can put in all the new wiring and drywall and fresh coats of paint, but none of that really changes them. They keep hold of their nature, the way reptiles in cages keep hold of their nature, and everything that echoes inside them stays.

From the moment we moved in, I found myself unable to do my work, not the way I used to. I was good at it back then, or at least good enough. I could focus on a problem for hours to the exclusion of all else, following the code as if it were a native language, sussing out the flaws and the bugs and running them down like a terrier runs down a rat. But in my new desk in this new place, with the smell of fresh paint still thick in the air, the most I could manage some days was to stare at the screen from the time I sat down in the morning until the clock finally clicked over to five.

Of course, it didn't help that the light from the window fell directly across my screen every morning for the entire month of February, or that the big heating ducts up on the ceiling made a click click clicking as they cooled, or that when all else was quiet you could hear the faint skitter of rats beneath the floorboards. And Ryan! Ryan, with his heavy heels like a spastic drum solo on the floorboards every time he talked on the phone. My sensitivities to such things always struck me as unreasonable, and I did my best to navigate them in silence.

Clearly, I was less than successful, but I want you to know that I tried.

I'm sure you noticed the drop in my productivity, and the fact that you said nothing about it was a real kindness to me. Or was it only that you had so many other things to focus on, what with the heavy weight of Tara's death and with Simmons being gone? Whatever the reason, it gave me space to find new ways to cope. I went on long walks away from my desk when the outside world became too much to bear. I hid myself away in the bathroom stalls. I climbed the stairs between our office and the unfinished half of the building, taking the steps slowly down and working my way back up again in the vain hope that I could burn away whatever nervous energy had taken hold of me. Nothing worked. The place continued to take its toll.

It's odd, isn't it, how simple decisions have such far-reaching consequences. I was drawn to those steps by the very fact that they were unfinished, that I could feel the original wood planking beneath my feet and see the old scorch marks still high on the walls where the sheets of new particleboard ended. Simmons would walk those stairs too, in those days before. I'd sometimes pass him on my way down, him huffing and out of breath as he hauled himself up by the handrail. I never mentioned that to you or to the police because at the time I had no idea.

But all this is preamble. I set out to explain to you why I can no longer stay in this place, and I promise that I will do exactly that. I do this as much for my own sake as for yours. Without this account they will say it was because I could no longer stand the place now that Tara was gone. They will gossip about all the time I used to spend hovering around her desk, trying to make her laugh. They will say that I was in love with her, and they will be right.

When she died, it was as if a hole had been ripped through the very fabric of the place. I know you felt it. Everyone did, and I'm not so delusional as to believe that the grief at her passing belonged to me alone. Worse, the suddenness of it, the sheer senselessness of someone with all her boundless life ahead of her being cut down in an alley for nothing more than the cash in her pocket and the silver bracelet on her wrist made the tragedy of it so much more acute. It was as if a mirror had been held up to our own mortality. If violence and death could come to someone so vibrant, so beautiful, then it could come for any of us, and we were all of us powerless to stop it.

Is that the reason that such a hush fell over the place after Simmons disappeared? It hadn't occurred to me until this moment, but the more I think on it the more certain I am that it must be the case. He'd been gone three days before the police came with their questions and the evidence boxes they used to carry away all his belongings. It was as if we all knew then that he wouldn't be back, that he was lost to us the same way that Tara had been lost to us. Only, with Tara we had the comfort of believing that her body was safe in her grave, her fate certain. Simmons was just gone.

I did not speak to Simmons in that time after Tara died. I saw him only once, at the door to that old stairwell. His eyes were dark and furtive, as if he feared to be followed. For his sake (or was it my own?) I made sure that I did not follow him, that he didn't even know I had seen him. It seemed to me then that he was grieving every bit as much as I. It seemed to me then that I was not the only one who had been in love with her.

Did you ever look into the history of this building before we bought it? Did anyone? Did you know that it stood vacant for more than ten years after the fire? That it sat, abandoned, a hollowed-out shell in the middle of the city that no one ever seemed to notice was there? It became a ghost long before our little company ever came into existence. Did anyone stop to question why it was we were able to purchase it so cheaply?

It was more than a week after the police came before I could bring myself to use those stairs again. It seemed absurd at the time, but there was a part of me that feared that I might find Simmons, lying in rot at the bottom, legs broken and starved, with all the soft parts of his face chewed away by the rats. I tried in vain to push the thought away, but it grew roots and dug in deep until all I could think about were the eyeless holes in his face staring up at me, pleading for me to find him. That the police had already checked the stairwell and found no sign of him mattered not at all. I'd close my eyes and the vision would be there, an afterimage burned against the insides of my eyelids. I would find no peace until I had been there, until I had seen the place for myself.

Of course, there was nothing. I had known that there would be nothing from the moment my foot touched the first step. And yet, in my bones I still knew that my business with that place was not done. Even now, this is the part I have trouble explaining to myself, and I hesitate to attempt to explain it to you now, because there's almost nothing of it that I truly understand. I can only say that the stairwell drew me to it the way a cold sore in the mouth draws the tongue, the way the needle draws the addict. I kept returning, not knowing what I expected to find there, but knowing still that I expected something. Over and over I climbed those steps, running my hands along the rough seams between the construction boards, searching for something, never knowing what.

It doesn't surprise me that the police didn't discover it. In fact, it took me more than a dozen trips up and down those stairs, each time a nagging voice at the back of my mind whispering to me that something was just not right, before I found the answer. The sheets of particleboard that made up the walls of the stairwell were fastened to the old wooden beams with long, black screws. It was hasty work, but solid, and left not so much as a single gap wide enough to let an insect through.

Only now, there was a gap! I found it in the corner of the first-floor landing, where a piece of wood had been cut down to fill the odd space barely two feet wide. There was something in the way the shadows fell across its edge that drew my eye, and when I ran my fingers along it, I found that it hung loose enough on one side for me to find a place to grip. I could see then that I was not the first to do so, as there were splinters and scratch marks at that very spot, as if it had been worried free with a screwdriver or a pocket knife. The board came away in my hands. It had never been screwed into place, but only fitted snug when it was installed. Beyond it was a void, as black and forbidding as the doorway to hell itself.

No doubt it is at this point where you would ask me why I didn't immediately climb the stairs and tell you, tell someone, what it was that I had found. It is a fair question, and one for which I have no answer. Perhaps it was the little thrill that filled me at the prospect of finding something that even the police had missed, for surely this passage had been long in use before they arrived. Perhaps it was my hope that it was nothing at all, that my imagination had been consumed with Simmons' disappearance and that my obsession had blossomed into paranoia. Whatever the reason, I pulled my phone from my pocket and, using it for a flashlight, crouched low and stepped into the space beyond the threshold.

At once I was able to stand again and, sensing the vast size of the space around me, turned my little light toward the ceiling. There I could see the wide gaps in the floor above where the fire had done its work, the old timbers bent low and charred white like old bones. The brickwork of the outside wall, still solid, was blackened with soot. The rounded arches of the window openings were boarded shut with new wood, like false teeth in a rotten mouth. All around me was ash and piles of charred wood, and the very air still smelled of the burning.

There was a scrap of nylon rope tied to a nail at the back of the loose board, inviting me to pull it shut behind me. I could not, because to do so would be like walling myself up inside my own tomb, and I will confess to you now that I was afraid of that place. My heartbeat was pounding in my throat, and how my curiosity won out over my instinct for self-preservation, I will never know. I was dimly aware of my feet pulling me forward, as if they had intentions of their own. Soon, I saw tracks in the layer of ash, a path that had been tamped down solid by the passage of footsteps and time. It led through a half-fallen doorway and around a corner where I could not see.

Again, the sensible part of me pleaded for me to turn back, and still my feet disobeyed. It was no longer fear that drove me, but excitement, excitement that I might discover at last what had become of Simmons, that in doing so I might be free of this strange obsession.

I stepped through the broken doorway. A low table had been propped there along the charred inner wall, little more than a jumble of burnt boards propped up by loose bricks. Seated next to it in a broken office chair was a silhouette in the shape of a human being. It gave me a start, but as soon as my light fell upon it, I could see that it was only the top half of a mannequin. Half its face was melted away, no doubt another casualty of the old fire. Where it had not burned, its plastic skin was cracked and yellowed, but still it kept an almost regal bearing, its head held high, aloof to its surroundings and its missing parts.

I approached the makeshift table, but halted as soon as I saw the objects arrayed upon it. There was the bundle of dried flowers: lilies and carnations taken from the arrangements that accumulated in Tara's cubicle in the week after her death. There was the little white teddy bear, now soiled and gray, that had once sat upon her desk. Among them was a scattering of photographs, most of them copies of the little wallet-sized portrait that her family had given us all after the funeral. But there were other photos there too, candid photos that could only have been taken without her knowledge. Photos taken on the street, Tara glancing furtively over one shoulder. Photos taken at a distance through a bedroom window. And there, upon that grotesque mannequin's outstretched wrist, the little silver bracelet.

It was here that I resolved to return to you, I swear. I wanted nothing more than to run from that place, to bring you, to bring the police, to expose Simmons and quit this strange hideaway and the half-finished stairs once and for all. But I could not. My feet remained rooted to the spot, and no matter how hard I tried I could not pull them away, for in that moment I knew that Simmons had never left that place. He was there with me, somewhere in the dark. I could hear the echoes of his shuffling footsteps. I could hear the rattling of his labored breaths.

Before I knew what I was doing, I found myself moving toward the sound. Even as I listened to the rhythm of his breathing I was dimly aware of some drive within myself, a latent survival instinct that told me that I must be the first to confront him, that I must find him before he had a chance to find me. My foot brushed a loose plank, and I took it up with both hands, brandishing it over my shoulder like a baseball bat. There was a light beyond the far doorway, beyond the filing cabinet that lay on its side, battered and empty like an old beer can. Step by step I drew closer, summoning all my courage, until at last I stood within the opening.

Simmons was there, just as I knew he would be. He had wrapped a dusty sheet of clear plastic around his gaunt frame like a shroud, and he fell to his knees like a supplicant at prayer. A layer of brick had been torn away from the wall, revealing a hidden alcove in the space beyond, an archway that had escaped the fire and shone now with a strange inner light, purple and shifting, with no apparent source.

It was this light that drew me forward. I forgot the board, and the sound of it echoed in the emptiness as it clattered to the floor behind me. Simmons paid it no mind, if he even heard it at all. He gave no sign of knowing that he was not alone. He was lost to the rhythmic swaying of his body, to the low sounds of his breath buzzing in his throat. There was movement inside the light from the alcove, shadows that seemed to dart and wheel within it like moths around a streetlamp. I stared at those shadows in their turnings. The lights had taken hold of me, and I surrendered myself to them.

Only then did I become dimly aware that the throaty rattle that Simmons made was not mere breathing but a chant. Over and over he said the words that barely seemed like words at all. Y'ai'ng'ngah, Yog-Sothoth. h'ee-l'geb f'ai throdog uaaah. Y'ai'ng'ngah, Yog-Sothoth. h'ee-l'geb f'ai throdog uaaah!

And as he chanted, the light from the alcove began to brighten, and it was as if I was no longer looking at a space on the wall but rather through a window. And in the emptiness beyond the alcove I could see bright spheres of yellow and white, pulsing in time with the words, swirling in their orbits, tugging at each other as if they were connected by invisible rubber bands.

Y'AI'NG'NGAH, YOG-SOTHOTH. H'EE-L'GEB F'AI THRODOG UAAAH!

At the sound of his upraised cry, I was at last able to tear myself away from the sight of those terrible, wondrous lights. In my trance I had stepped forward and was now standing next to Simmons, close enough to touch, as he rocked and shuddered on the floor. He turned his gaze to me. There, framed in its dirty plastic shawl, at last I could see his face.

I ran from the place then, heedless of the cinders that scattered beneath my feet and the high wail of terror that escaped my throat. I nearly threw myself out of the opening beneath the stairs, certain that, were I to so much as look over my shoulder I would see his terrible visage staring back at me. But he did not follow. I ran back up the steps, taking them two at a time for fear that he would be right there on my heels, but when I reached the top, my heart thudding in my chest, I was alone.

I told no one of what I had seen. I returned to my desk, and here I have sat all through the night since then, staring into the black mirror of my monitor screen, not daring to speak, barely daring to breathe. It was only as the first threads of dawn began to filter through the windows that I finally mustered the courage to return to that place. Simmons was gone. So too was the shrine he had made, the makeshift table destroyed, the mannequin lying in pieces on the floor. In the ashes I found a single, tiny photograph. Tara smiling in those carefree days that were long gone now. I carry it in my pocket even now.

The alcove is still there, though its lights have gone dark. I urge you to see it for yourself, after the authorities have had their say. Take note of the long marks that Simmons' fingernails made in the crumbling mortar, of the nest he had made for himself out of insulation and rotting cloth, of the piles of dead rats with their insides bitten out. Take note of the ageworn inscriptions on the old walls, but do not look long.

I fear that they will take root in your mind the way they have taken root in mine.

Why, I ask you! Why did no one consider the history of this place before we came here? Why did no one stop to question how eight people died in a fire where none of the doors had been locked!

And when you see that place, take note of the footprints, still visible in the powdery ash. They end at the base of the alcove, Simmons' steps heavy and dragging. And next to them, a second set of prints, barefoot and small, tracing a delicate path beside them.

But my time has come. You have left the office and I have just watched the door close behind you. I am on my way to the roof, now. If I see you in the parking lot, I will wave to you before I go. I only wish that I could have told you all of this in person, that you could see the truth of it written on my face. But I cannot risk you changing my mind. I cannot risk the chance of having to mourn her all over again. You've been a good boss, and for the most part I am happy to have worked here. Do not allow any of this to convince you otherwise.

I've left my password on a piece of paper taped to the bottom of my keyboard. Evelyn can take care of the rest. And if you have occasion to meet Simmons again, do not look into his eyes! There are infinities there that you cannot fathom.

Thank you, and goodbye.

C.

A Candle for the Birthday Boy

THE KID WAS TURNING six, and he was missing the whole thing.

Not that it mattered to him, Nate thought. What did six year-olds know about what it took to throw a party this size, about what it cost to keep over a hundred kids full of cake and punch when the guest of honor was off hiding who knows where? What did he care that they were all waiting, waiting for him to come outside and open the presents that their parents had spent far too much money on in hopes of impressing his old man? The party was almost over and he couldn't even be bothered to come out of the house.

No, that wasn't fair. Danny was only a kid, after all. He shouldn't have to worry about things like money and all the pressures that came with it. Besides, Tabby was the one he should be angry at. He hadn't seen her all day either, and she was supposed to be responsible for half this mess. He had counted on her to be here, to fill the glasses with punch, to cut the cake and pretend she cared about the kid. A few of the single mothers in attendance had noticed her absence, or at least sensed it in his thoughts the way sharks smelled blood in open water. The quick among them were all too happy to step in, the whole time casting sidelong glances at him that said that they'd be willing to take over for Tabitha at more than just the cake table.

As much as he wanted to, as much as he saw her absence as the excuse he needed, he felt guilty for being mad at her. This whole thing, this party, had been her idea, and as soon as she'd brought it up, he'd wrapped all his hopes around it. It was the first time in the eight months they had been together that she had shown anything better than disdain for the little boy, and he was not about to let it slip away. Nate had seen the way she looked at Danny sometimes, with that absent, almost vacant stare, like she was looking at an animal she'd just as soon put to sleep. He had wanted to see this new offer as a gesture, as a sign that she had accepted the boy, that she was willing to take the two of them as a unit, and see herself as part of a family. Now, he wasn't so sure what he wanted.

She had had everything ready by the time he was out of bed. The thoughtfulness, the sheer amount of selfless activity, was so uncharacteristic of her that he should have suspected it right away. She had clipped down the tablecloths and stocked the plates. She had filled the punch bowl and covered it with plastic wrap to keep out the bugs. And though the idea of assigned seats evaporated once the children arrived, she had even taped down place cards.

And, of course, there was the piñata.

She had tied it to a tree near the center of the yard. It hung there, big and garish, an eyesore in the shape of a bloated sheep. Alternating bands of green and yellow worked their way forward from its rump, culminating in a grin and cartoon eyes that were far too big for the proportions of its head. It was hideous, but she had insisted upon the thing, telling him that, in her family, it was a birthday tradition.

There was that word again: family. She had used it expertly, wielding it like a weapon pointed straight at his heart. He'd wanted to object, but she had played him and she had won, just like she always did.

A fat child stalked by the cake table, drinking what must have been his fourth cup of punch. He walked by the piñata, eyeing it hungrily. He and the other children were restless, hopped up on sugar and anticipation. Nate wished, not for the first time, that Sandra was there. Sandra would have known what to do. Sandra would have been able to keep this party from disintegrating into a riot. Sandra would have been able to make her son, their son, show up for his own birthday.

But Sandra was in Colorado. Nate had seen to that. He had driven her away and replaced her with a pale imitation. A younger imitation, to be sure. One that looked better in a black, see-through nightgown and knew a few extra tricks between the sheets. One who scared him sometimes with the feral look that seemed to come over her like a storm when he least expected it. One who had once taken a carving knife out of the kitchen drawer and pointed it at his throat from across the room.

At the end of the lawn, the magician he had hired for two hundred dollars an hour was twisting balloons into shapes while a crowd of distracted children sat bouncing their legs on the grass. Their mothers stood behind them, forming a corral with their bodies and trying to not be too obvious as they checked their watches.

He tried to picture Sandra, working the crowd, engaging the mothers as only another woman with children could. He tried to remember her walk, the way she moved. He tried to picture her face, but all he could see was Tabitha, that wild animal look in her eyes as she screamed at him, screamed threats and obscenities that made his muscles tense and his cheeks turn hot. All he could see was her lithe form blocking the doorway as he tried to walk away, a mist of spittle and dark intentions spraying from her mouth like venom until finally his hand rang across her face and left her eyes wide with silent shock.

But that was weeks ago, one shameful moment best left forgotten. He had wanted to end things with Tabitha then, just call it off and send her packing, but she had thrown herself into the planning of the party with such enthusiasm that he all but forgot about it. She had meant for him to forget it. He wasn't naïve enough to believe otherwise and he wasn't naïve enough to believe she had forgotten his part in it either. But he had seen such sincerity in her actions, a genuine wish to make amends, that he could not refuse. Only now, alone among all these people, did he begin to see the cruel joke she had played on him.

He handed another cup full of punch to a little girl who took it and turned away without saying a word. She had to stop to let the fat kid by as he shouldered across her path. Nate had the kid figured right away: awkward, spoiled, a bully in training. His route took him in long, leisurely arcs around the piñata, circling it like a hyena stalking a wounded gazelle. He tried to look disinterested, all the while alternating his gaze between the stick, left tantalizingly against the trunk of the tree, and the one person in sight with the authority to keep him from picking it up and bashing the hanging prize to papery bits. Nate met the kid's gaze with a silent warning, and watched him skulk away to join the others.

He cast a glance back at the house, hoping that his son was somewhere inside, just pouting over his mother. He tried not to listen to the gnawing animal in his gut that told him he wasn't. Tabby was gone. That much he was sure of. Knowing it should have left him relieved, after everything, so why was the thought mixed in with so much dread? She wouldn't take the boy with her. She hated Danny. He knew that now. She hated Danny almost as much as Nate realized she had grown to hate him. Would she take Danny just to get back at him for what he'd done? Was she even capable of something like that?

Again, the feral face returned to him, the knife flashing beneath it in the dim glow of nighttime. Oh yes, came the answer. She's capable of that. She's capable of all that and worse.

He turned back to the piñata, that grinning monstrosity that seemed to taunt him with the punch-line of a joke that it wasn't willing to share. He looked at the wide, hemp rope tied around its middle, and only now noticed that it was tied like a noose.

He looked across the crowd of children, touching every face with his eyes, hoping with growing panic that the next one they fell upon would be the face of his boy. One by one he passed them, and with each one he felt a tingle rise higher up his spine and tighten across his scalp. How long had Tabby been gone?

Five, maybe six hours at most? In that time she couldn't have gotten far. He had to call the police. He would call them and they would find her. They would take her away in handcuffs and the boy would come leaping into his arms. They would lock her away and the two of them would be free and he could call Sandra and maybe they could start all over again.

He put a hand on the table to steady himself. A fly landed on his knuckle and he paused to bat it away. He couldn't call the police, not yet. What if Danny was just hiding after all? What if he was just playing a game of hide and seek with some of the other kids and hid so well that they'd lost interest and stopped looking? He knew the thought was stupid, but it calmed him anyway. He couldn't call the police until he was sure, and before he could be sure he had to go back into the house. Someone else could watch the party. The party could go straight to Hell for all he cared, as long as he found the boy.

"Hey! Put that down!"

Nate turned to see a woman in a red dress taking the fat kid by the arm. Was she his mother, or someone else's mother? Nate didn't care. The stick was in the kid's hand, and now he dropped it to the ground and stomped away. High above the scene, the piñata grinned.

How long are you going to wait? it seemed to say. How long before you go back into the house and find out what you already know? Tabby's gone. Long gone. But the boy might still be there, somewhere. She wouldn't have taken him because she hated him even more than she ended up hating you, but that doesn't mean you won't still find him there, in the house, left someplace where it won't take you too long to stumble across his body.

A breeze kicked up, brushing another fly past his nose. The leaves in the tree swayed, but the piñata was like an anchor at the end of its rope. That insane, wide-eyed face still pointed right at him, and beyond him to the house. *Go on,* he heard it say in Tabitha's voice. *Go back to the house. Go back and see what I've left there for you.*

More children swarmed the punchbowl, helping themselves now that Nate was no longer keeping up. He barely noticed them. His eyes were fixed on the piñata, on the wicked grin that still seemed to be keeping secrets.

"Here, let me help."

Nate heard the voice, but it wasn't until he felt the hand gently taking the ladle away from him that he actually turned to see who had spoken. He didn't know her name, but he recognized the windblown blonde hair that spilled out from dark roots to her shoulders. She was pretty in spite of her hair, and she didn't have a wedding ring. None of the mothers here seemed to have wedding rings. He would have noticed the expectant smile on her face, but he was looking past her, at the house.

"Could you..." he began. The sentence didn't have an ending that would make him seem anything but crazy. Could you call the police? Could you send everyone home so I can hunt down my girlfriend? Could you keep the children out of the house in case my son is lying dead inside?

"I just need to go check on something," he said finally. "In the house."

"I'll be waiting," she said, and he would have picked up on the flirtation in her tone, maybe even enjoyed it, if she hadn't sounded so far away. He moved past her, more conscious with every step of the cartoon eyes that bored into his back. That piñata, that monstrosity, would be watching him the whole way, never wavering, never moving, not even swaying in the wind.

The thought stopped him, and he turned. As if on cue, the wind kicked up again. Paper plates tumbled off tables and napkins took wing. Leaves swayed back and forth, moving with the air.

The piñata didn't budge.

Once again he started toward the house, this time determined to make it there without looking back. Tabitha had hung the piñata there to unnerve him, to make him panic. He wasn't about to let it do either of those things. The house was where he needed to focus. The house was where he needed to be. He couldn't let the image of the thing's grin cloud his thinking. It was paper, that was all. Paper and paste in the shape of an animal.

But if it was just paper, why didn't it move with the wind? If there was only candy inside, why did it need such a thick piece of rope to hold it in the air?

In the distance behind him, he heard a commotion that made him stop again. The house was close now. Less than a dozen yards and he would be inside. Still, the upraised voices made him all the more certain that he could not go inside, that he wasn't running toward the things that he dreaded discovering, but away from them.

The children were running now. He could see them at the edges of his vision. He turned his head to watch them, knowing why they were running, and knowing where their paths would all meet. Their mothers chased them, but they couldn't keep up. They called out, but the children did not hear.

The fat kid had the stick. He swung it in wide, scything motions so that no one dared get close enough to take it away from him. Mothers shouted, but his eyes were fixed on the prize. The children crowded around, just outside the reach of his swing, as he brought the stick up and over his head. A scream welled up in Nate's throat but couldn't find any breath to carry it.

The piñata grinned in triumph as the stick struck home.

The thing bobbed on its rope like a man dropped from a gallows. A cloud of flies scattered, only to close back upon it as the fat kid hefted the stick for another swing. The children held their breath, waiting to see what would spill out. Nate held his breath too, knowing all too well what it would be. Already he could see the dark stain where the stick had cracked the paper, spreading out across the green and yellow in a blossom of brownish red.

Again, Nate tried to scream. His feet were moving, and all his breath seemed to be used up in the motion. The fat kid was grinning, almost manic. He held the stick above him like an executioner's axe, and Nate could see now that the edge of it was thin and sharp, like a blade. His eyes were wide, his teeth set, and in that grimace, Nate could almost see the echo of Tabitha's face, laughing at him.

Then the stick struck again and the piñata spilled its contents in a slush upon the ground.

The children tensed for an instant, ready to pounce. Then they froze. Their shoulders drooped as they saw the glistening aftermath at their feet and, instinctively, they stepped away. Mothers stood behind them, their mouths hanging open. The fat kid dropped the stick, and looked down at the blood that covered his shoes. In the crowd, one of the children started to cry.

Nate staggered to his knees at the edge of the puddle of gore, and though grief filled his chest the way the heady scent filled his nostrils, all his mind could do was to ask itself over and over what he was going to say. What would he say to the children who stood slack-jawed, to their mothers who looked at him with accusation in their eyes? What would he say to Sandra when he told her what he had allowed to happen? Most importantly, what was he going to say to Tabitha once he got his hands around her throat?

The head of the piñata dangled above him, still grinning, bobbing at the end of the rope. It dripped out the rest of its contents in a steady rhythm upon the grass. *How could there be more of it?* There was already so much on the ground. There was too much. There was far too much.

Then he looked at what lay in front of him, really looked for the first time. There was a liver, too large, like a half-inflated beach ball. There was a length of tripe, and a smashed, spongy mass that might once have been sweetbreads. A pig's head lolled on its side, severed by the butcher's saw just below the jaw line. Its feet poked up at odd angles from piles of meat and bone. In the middle of it all, soaked through with blood, was a pair of Danny's overalls.

Nate looked up at the grinning head of the piñata, and through his tears, he began to laugh.

"Daddy?"

He turned, and Danny was there. He stood, whole and alive. The sun shone bright upon his dark hair, and he was smiling. Then he saw the tears in his father's eyes, the mass of meat and entrails beyond him. His face fell, and his body began to shake. Nate pulled him close, and held on as hard as he could.

"Daddy..."

"It's all right, son."

"Aunt Tabby told me to hide in the house. She told me to wait until the piñata broke open, and then I could come out."

"I know, son. It's all right."

The boy's voice was quickly turning to sobs. "It was a joke, daddy. I didn't know what was inside. Aunt Tabby told me that it would be funny."

"Aunt Tabby was wrong." *She was wrong, all right*, Nate thought. When he finally caught up with her, he'd make sure she knew just how wrong she had been.

"I'm sorry, daddy."

Nate held the child out at arms' length. "It's not your fault, son."

Tears began to dry on the child's cheeks. "You're not mad?"

"I'm not mad."

Danny's mood seemed to change on a dime, and a smile spread across his face. The others seemed on their way to forgetting too, because Nate could hear the sounds of nervous conversation beginning all around him. He would make them understand that none of this had been his idea, that Tabby was the one to blame for all of it. He would clean up the mess, then he would call Sandra and tell her he was sorry, sorry for everything. He would ask her, he would beg her, to come back from Colorado, so they could be a family again. She would come back, and everything would be all right.

"Can I go play now, daddy?"

Nate ran his hand through the child's hair, gaining strength from the warmth that he felt there. "Of course you can."

Danny turned and was off as if nothing had happened. He snagged a cup of punch from the long table as he went, and the other children trailed off to follow. Nate looked up at the mothers who lingered near the piñata, and he was pleased to see that the looks on their faces were ones of sympathy, and not accusation. Perhaps everything really was going to be just fine.

He stood and walked back to the punch bowl, basking in the sense of normalcy he felt as he took his place behind it. Some had spilled in the commotion, and the puddle was finding its way onto the grass in small drips. He'd clean it up later, he thought. He'd clean everything up later. He threw a napkin down at the edge of the table to stop the dripping, and only then did he notice that in the middle of the sticky pool lay a crowd of dead flies.

Across the yard, Danny ran in a circle with his friends. They stopped running, and the boy raised the cup to his lips. Nate felt all his fear and dread return as if they had never left, and he cried out to his son to stop him.

But it was too late. The cup was almost empty, and all around him, children were starting to fall.

About the Author

Born and raised near the shores of Lake Michigan, Christopher Hawkins has been writing and telling stories for as long as he can remember. A dyed-in-the-wool geek, he is an avid collector of books, roleplaying games and curiosities. When he's not writing, he spends his time exploring old cemeteries, lurking in museums, and searching for a decent cup of tea.

Christopher is the former editor of the One Buck Horror anthology series. His works of short fiction have been published in numerous magazines and anthologies, including Read By Dawn vol 2, The Big Book of New Short Horror, Fusion Fragment, Underland Arcana and Cosmic Horror Monthly. He is a member of the Chicago Writers Association and the Chicagoland chapter of the Horror Writers Association.

An expatriate Hoosier, Christopher currently lives in a suburb of Chicago with his wife and two sons.

www.christopher-hawkins.com

Acknowledgments

Books, especially short story collections, are never created in a vacuum. They're the result of a thousand serendipitous events and little acts of kindness that, in the aggregate, give a writer confidence that he can embark on such an unlikely undertaking and make it work. This book is the sum of those acts and those events, and I am incredibly grateful for each and every one of them.

Thanks to Sadie Hartmann for her early and unwavering support. Thanks to Brian Asman, John Everson, Eric LaRocca, Christi Nogle and Brian Pinkerton for lending their kind and supportive words. Thanks to Alan Lastufka for advice that helped to smooth the treacherous waters of the publishing sea. Thanks to Brandy Schwan for witchy research assistance and to Fay Lane and Emily Kardamis for their design expertise.

Thanks to Benjamin and Timothy for putting up with their dad, both in general and specific to this project, and for helping me to not take any of this too seriously. Thanks to Kris for being my rock, and the grounding wire that keeps my neurotic electricity from burning the whole place down. I love you all.

Thanks to the group at the Chicago chapter of the Horror Writers Association for being a beacon to follow and a place to belong. Thanks to Becky Spratford for dragging me (kicking and screaming) out of my shell. Thanks to Lauren Bolger for being one of the first to believe in this book.

Lastly, tremendous thanks to each and every one of the editors and publishers who originally published these stories. Without their belief in my work, I might have stopped before I could ever get started. I'm glad that I didn't.

Christopher Hawkins
February, 2023

Thirsty for more?

If you enjoyed this book, the stories don't have to end here. There's more waiting for you at **suburbanmonsters.com/free**. Just scan the QR Code below, or visit the website to claim your **FREE** bonus ebook!

www.suburbanmonsters.com/free

Made in the USA
Monee, IL
17 June 2023